By the same author:

**STEPHANIE
STEPHANIE'S CASTLE
STEPHANIE'S DOMAIN
STEPHANIE'S REVENGE
STEPHANIE'S TRIAL
STEPHANIE'S PLEASURE**

**MELINDA AND THE MASTER
MELINDA AND ESMERALDA
MELINDA AND THE COUNTESS**

MELINDA AND THE ROMAN

Susanna Hughes

Nexus

This book is a work of fiction.
In real life, make sure you practise safe sex.

First published in 1995 by
Nexus
332 Ladbroke Grove
London W10 5AH

Copyright © Susanna Hughes 1995

Typeset by TW Typesetting, Plymouth, Devon
Printed and bound in Great Britain by
Cox & Wyman Ltd, Reading, Berks

ISBN 0 352 32972 6

All characters in this publication are fictitious and any resemblance to real persons, living or dead, is purely coincidental.

This book is sold subject to the condition that it shall not, by way of trade or otherwise, be lent, resold, hired out or otherwise circulated without the publisher's prior written consent in any form of binding or cover other than that in which it is published and without a similar condition including this condition being imposed on the subsequent purchaser.

One

Melinda pressed her body against the mirror, squashing her firm, round breasts almost flat, her bulbous nipples trapped between the cold glass and her ribs. She was naked apart from a pair of plain black panties that clung tightly to her flat navel and the tight, neat curves of her buttocks.

She was being watched. Though she had no way of knowing, she felt it instinctively. Someone behind the mirror was watching her through the two-way glass. Pulling away, her eyes staring intently at their own jade-green reflection, she cupped her breasts in her hands, squeezing the pliant flesh between her fingers until it was white, and she felt a pang of pain that became a rush of pleasure. She pushed her breasts up towards her chin so she could see the little purple squares, the colour of indelible ink, with which she had been marked. Centred under each breast the squares both contained the letter M – Melinda and the Master.

She was hot. Sweat beaded her body, running over her navel and into the silky material of the panties, darkening them further around the waistband. There was sweat on her long, dimpled and contoured thighs too, a thin film of sweat that made her skin glisten.

Letting her breasts drop, she laced her fingers

together behind her neck so she could get an unobstructed view of her body. She raised herself on tiptoe, as if she were wearing high heels, so the muscles of her legs were shaped and firm. She *was* beautiful. Very beautiful. She wanted to be so beautiful for her new Master. Her breasts were not large but were full and high. Her waist was narrow and the flare of her hips generous, giving her an hourglass figure. She half-turned so she could see her pert, apple-shaped arse, covered in a triangle of clinging black nylon. The crease where the top of her thighs tucked under her buttocks was deep, an almost perfect crescent on both sides. The cleft between her buttocks was deep too, a gorge that the black silky material had been sucked into.

She turned back to face the mirror again, allowing her heels to rest on the floor. She looked at her flat navel bisected by the panties, and the way – here, too – the material seemed to have been drawn up into the furrow of her sex.

Though her flaxen blonde and very wavy hair was not long she held it up so she could see the sinews of her long neck. She stared into her face. Her green eyes looked back at her quizzically, their whites clear and unblemished, her eyelashes noticeably long. Her cheekbones were round and her nose small and slightly retroussé. Her mouth was not large but she had full pouting lips that were naturally a deep ruby red.

As she dropped her hands to her sides she watched how the movement made her breasts quiver. Her nipples were disproportionately large in comparison to the surrounding mass especially when, as now, they were erect, the corrugated flesh as hard as stone.

She traced a line from the hollow of her throat,

down between her breasts to the waistband of the panties, where her hand burrowed underneath, distending the material. She would never have dared do this before, never have tried to touch herself without permission, but Esmeralda – the girl she had been chained to constantly by her second Master – had told her it was allowed. Between Masters, being delivered from one to another, often from one country to another, the slaves were in a sort of limbo, the reigns of control slackened, until the formality of delivery was complete.

Even knowing this, Melinda had never allowed herself to be tempted before. But there had never been a mirror before, never been the opportunity to look at her near naked body before, nor the provocation of knowing that, behind it, other eyes were staring at her. It might even be her new Master.

That thought excited her more. She saw a flame of passion dance in her eyes as the tips of her fingers brushed against the fleece of her pubic hair. She had been made to shave her hair away but it had regrown slightly although no more than a soft short stubble. Her middle finger delved down until she could feel the slit of her labia. She pushed into it, under the little hood of flesh, to unveil her clitoris. It was engorged and wet.

Her left hand went back to her breast, thumb and forefinger pinching at each nipple in turn. She watched in the mirror, her eyes narrowing slightly at each surge of pain as her fingernails bit deep into the sensitive tissue. She felt her clitoris throb against her finger. Taking her left nipple she stretched it, pulling her breast out like a piece of rubber, as if to see how far it would go. Suddenly and deliberately, she let it go, her breast falling back, another surge of sensation coursing through her and churning up the feelings in her clit.

She sank to her knees in front of the mirror, her thigh muscles taut and broad in this position. Her legs were open, the wide plane of her sex completely covered by the panties, the material dimpled where it stuck to the contours of her labia.

Staring into the mirror, she tried to imagine who was behind the glass, tried to envisage whose eyes were watching her. Was it her new Master, the man who would rule her life for the next three months? Was he there on his own, standing watching her with a drink in his hand, assessing her objectively as one might a newly acquired painting? Or was he naked, his cock excited by what he had seen, watching her intently, eyes moving over every detail of her body, her beauty fuelling his desire, hand pumping his erection? There was a third possibility, of course: that he was not alone. The hand that circled his cock was not his own but one of his slaves', his favourite perhaps, brought along especially, just in case the new arrival should provoke the Master's desire.

Melinda's eyes stared intently as if trying to burn away the silvering of the mirror and reveal the enigma beyond.

She had moved her left hand down to the back of the panties, while the right still teased at her clitoris. Diving down under the silky nylon, she followed the cleft of her buttocks until she could feel the little wrinkled crater of her anus. Like all the main orifices of her body it had been extensively used by the Masters. The tip of her finger flirted with her sphincter but did not penetrate inside. Instead she moved her hand lower until her fingers were between her thick labia at the mouth of her sex. She shuddered as she felt her own heat and wetness.

In the mirror she looked at her body, one arm twisted behind her back, the crotch of the panties lumpy and stretched by her fingers, breasts trembling slightly, nipples prominent. She had been ordered to masturbate in front of her Master and had hated it, craving his touch instead. But this was different. This was a performance, a demonstration, her chance to advertise her wares and make him believe she was special.

She crawled forward until her knees touched the bottom of the mirror. She pushed her chest out until her nipples brushed the glass. It was only then she pushed two, then three, fingers deep into the glutinous heat of her sex.

'Oh . . .' escaped her lips.

She gazed into her green eyes, the reflection and the reality only inches apart now. She could see her own need, bright and greedy.

Her finger worked on her clit – moving it from side to side, pressing it hard against her pubic bone – while she eased her fingers out to the bottom of her vagina, then stabbed them back in again, penetrating as deep as they would go, feeling the soft, spongy flesh parting. She wished it was a cock invading her, the Master's cock, wished the mirror would melt away and her new Master would take her, ravish her. She tried to pretend, tried to imagine the heat and smoothness and rigidity of a big phallus buried inside her, throbbing and hot, ready to jerk and spit out its spunk.

'Oh . . .' she moaned loudly, pressing her breasts against the glass again; then her lips, kissing their reflection. 'Oh, Master . . .' The words left a trail of saliva on the mirror.

Her fingers pounded her clit relentlessly. She would

have liked to take the panties off, liked to watch her sex being violated by her own hand, the tendons of her knuckles stretched to the limit, but that she did not dare do. She contented herself with looking deep into her own eyes, watching the glints and refractions of light that shone out as a testament to her feelings.

A profound tremor ran through her body, the precursor to her climax. She jammed her three fingers deep and then straining the tendons of her hand even further, tried to spread them apart in the soft flesh that encased them. It was a wonderful sensation. Holding them there, she strummed at her clitoris, a light touch but much faster until she felt her nerves begin to knit together – interlacing, combining until they were one – then heaving her up over the precipice of orgasm and then down into the abyss beyond, where she could do nothing, think nothing, except experience the depths of raw pleasure.

The force of her climax had closed her eyes. When she opened them again it was almost like waking from a deep sleep and not knowing where she was. She was startled to see her eyes staring back at her from the mirror.

Just as surely as she knew someone had been watching, she now knew that they had gone. She was alone again.

The cell was hot, intensely so, and airless. There was only one small window set too high in the wall for her to be able to reach, and anyway, it was sealed and barred. There was no draught either from around the frame of the single heavy wooden door. The unplastered breezeblock walls seemed to radiate the heat back into the room. At night there was a certain coolness but, by midday, as the sun climbed high, the heat increased and the temperature in the cell became unbearable and stayed that way until long after the sun had set.

All of the cells in the halfway houses – where the slaves were held before being delivered to their new masters – were like this one, primitive and barely furnished. There was an upright wooden chair and a wooden-framed single bed with a thin mattress. The only other feature of the room was a large metal ring screwed securely into the beam that ran the width of the room. Attached to the ring was a short length of chain, at the end of which was a hook. None of the other cells had ever had a mirror, let alone a full-length one.

It was deliberate, of course. Melinda knew the ways of the members of *L'Organisation Internationale de Maîtres* well enough to know that everything that was done happened for a reason. With her previous Masters, a mirror had been a luxury she was not permitted. It was surplus to requirements. It implied that she was free to make decisions about her appearance, about what to wear, what make-up to use and how to do her hair, when in fact these decisions, like every other aspect of her life – from when she was fed to when she went to the bathroom – had been delegated, freely and willingly, to her Masters.

Only occasionally, and mostly by accident, had Melinda caught sight of herself in a mirror. It had usually been the face of a stranger that had greeted her, her hair styled differently, her make-up in different colours from any she would have used herself. Dressed for the Master's pleasure, her clothes too would be unfamiliar and, frankly, usually obscene.

She had come to accept it, even to welcome it, her life stripped of anything that would interfere with her desire to subjugate herself, to act and be the perfect slave. She did not belong to herself any more, she was a chattel, to be decorated and adorned like the object she was.

The mirror in the cell had therefore come as something of a shock. And its effect on her had been startling. With nothing else to do she had stared at her body as though it were a stranger and had been able to admire her beauty, so long unseen, with an objective eye. The truth was, what she saw in the mirror – the flaxen-haired, slender-bodied creature – had turned her on, had made her pulse with a sexual energy which was never far from the surface since she had become involved with the OIM.

The mirror had provoked her. In the other cells in the halfway houses she had been passive and had never wanted to masturbate. Which is why she knew placing the mirror in the room was deliberate, and why she was sure that it was a two-way glass from behind which she could be observed. When and by whom she had no way of knowing, but she had stood in front of it for hours on end, trying to fathom its mysteries.

She had been flown from Paris in a private jet, knowing only that her destination was Rome. The jet had been wheeled into a hangar before Melinda had been escorted off the plane and into a small panelled van for the journey to the halfway house.

That had been three days ago. Three days of stifling heat and the unchanging image of herself in the tall mirror – each day had been exactly the same. Woken by a surly brunette who looked as if she might once have been a shotputter for an Eastern European country and whose ill-fitting grey uniform threatened to burst its seam at any minute, Melinda was escorted down a short corridor to a primitive bathroom with a toilet and a bath and allowed to use both while the guard waited and watched. She was then returned to her cell, where fruit, bread and cheese had been laid on the bed with a plastic bottle of water. There she would be left all day until twilight when another visit to the bathroom had been supervised, after which more food was provided. Then she would be left again until morning.

It had been similar at all the halfway houses and again, Melinda was sure, represented a deliberate policy. It was as though the stultifying boredom was intended to ready the slave for the new Master, to allow her to think about all that had happened to her with her last Master and digest it mentally so she was properly ready for a new experience, the old slate wiped clean.

But it was not only a mental process but a physical one. After two or three days of almost total isolation, the body yearned for human contact. It was what Melinda missed most. It made even the smallest touch, the slightest suggestion of tenderness, seem incredibly important. A look from the Master, let alone a caress, would make her want to cry with gratitude. Any contact, even a merciless beating, was better than none at all.

As well as the boredom and isolation, there was fear. None of the slaves were ever told anything about their future, from minute to minute as well as from day to day, but Melinda had been told that her new Master was known for his cruelty. She feared what he might do to her, though it was a fear tinged with a delicious, almost tangible, sense of excitement. Melinda was, after all, a willing slave. Her submission satisfied a profound current in her psyche which she didn't wholly understand or want to understand. She only knew what she felt.

It was on the fourth day that the pattern changed. Melinda had been brought back to her cell and given her breakfast as usual, but then an hour later, though she had no way of telling precisely, the heavy key had ground in the lock and the cell door had swung open. The substantial figure of the guard stood in the doorway. She was accompanied by another very different type of woman who had walked into the cell ahead of her.

'Good morning, my dear,' she said in perfect English, though with a strong Italian accent.

The woman was beautiful. Her face – with high cheekbones, a very straight nose, a delicate chiselled chin and big dark-brown eyes – suggested an aristocratic pedigree. Her long black hair was pinned in a chignon to her head, which she held high, meeting the world with an assurance born of her experience. She was tall, slender and tanned, and dressed in the finest quality clothes – a body-hugging cream suit, its jacket buttoned with no blouse underneath. Her legs were sheathed, despite the heat, in almost transparent flesh-coloured nylons with a glass-like sheen. High-heeled cream shoes with a small gold Gucci motif completed her outfit. Her pose and elegance suited the expensive clothes perfectly. Her perfume was expensive, too; a heady scent had entered the cell with her.

'Oh yes, but you are beautiful,' she continued, looking at Melinda who was sitting on the bed. 'Up . . .' Her voice brooked no argument. She was clearly used to giving commands and having them obeyed.

Melinda got to her feet, her heart pounding, her excitement intense. It was not just the relief from boredom. Immediately Melinda had set eyes on the woman she had felt an entirely different emotion, undiluted lust, and it had taken her completely by surprise. Not that she hadn't felt desire for a woman before. She had, but could not recall it being so strong or overwhelming. This woman had a special quality, a strength and power which Melinda responded to at once.

'I am the wife of your new Master. My name is Sophia.' The woman walked around Melinda examining her body, her heels clacking on the stone floor, her nylons rasping slightly as she moved.

Melinda inhaled her perfume. It is said that most expensive scents have a different aroma with each wearer. The combination of this woman and her perfume produced an aroma that was heady with an unmistakable muskiness; the musk, at least for Melinda, of sex.

'You may go,' Sophia said to the guard, who retreated through the cell door immediately though grudgingly, perhaps regretting that she was not going to be allowed to watch. Melinda heard the door being locked behind her.

'He was right about you,' the woman mused. 'You are quite beautiful.' She had completed her circumnavigation and, once again, stood in front of Melinda, their eyes meeting for the first time. 'Aren't you?'

'Yes, mistress,' Melinda said, her voice croaky. They were the first words she had spoken in days.

'I would prefer you to call me mistress Sophia.'

'Yes, mistress Sophia,' Melinda intoned at once.

'Mmm ... I think you will be happy with us. My husband and I like to share everything, you understand. Everything.' It was unusual for a slave to be given any information, let alone this sort of detail. 'He does, however, leave punishment to me. That is something he cares to watch but not to administer. Fortunately I seem to have a penchant for it.' Melinda saw a spark flare in her eyes, like two flints struck together to produce fire. It was this woman, she knew at once, who had created her husband's reputation for cruelty. She felt the familiar *mélange* of fear and excitement.

'Tell me what you feel,' Sophia said quietly, sensing Melinda's emotions.

Melinda could not think of a single thing to say. In all her time with the Masters she had never been asked such a question. She was a slave, submissive, obedient, an object who was not supposed to have feelings.

'I asked you a question. You must answer,' Sophia said firmly.

Melinda could only express the truth. 'Desire, mistress Sophia.'

'Desire?'

'Yes, mistress Sophia.'

'Desire for me?'

'Yes, mistress Sophia.'

'I see.' She was stroking the fingers of one hand against her bottom lip. 'And why is that?' Sophia turned away from Melinda and looked into the mirror. An image of two women, as different from one another as any could be, greeted her gaze – one blonde and almost naked, the other brunette, coutured and coiffured, and yet both remarkably beautiful.

'You are very beautiful, mistress Sophia.'

'Take your panties down. Grasp your ankles in your hands, I'm sure you know the position . . .'

Melinda's heart skipped a beat. She was not just

being inspected casually. Sophia would not have ordered her into this position if she hadn't got something else in mind. Quickly Melinda pulled the black panties down over her legs and stepped out of them. She spread her legs apart and bent over, grasping her ankles firmly in her hands, the whole furrow of her sex tilted up and exposed, the thin growth of pubic hair covering nothing.

Sophia came up behind her.

'You have been shaved?'

'Yes, mistress Sophia.'

'But not recently.' Sophia's hand brushed against the fluffy hair on Melinda's labia.

'No, mistress Sophia.'

'I will have you shaved again.'

Sophia's touch was not as light this time. Her fingers delved into Melinda's labia, parting the thick lips to reveal the scarlet entrance to her vagina. Another finger probed inside. 'You're very wet, girl,' Sophia said. It was not a question. Melinda made no reply. She was not allowed to speak unless she was asked a question. That was the rule; it was common to all the Masters. The only other rule was unquestioning obedience to any command.

The finger probed deeper, bending at the joint to scratch the inner surfaces. Strangely, the woman's finger felt cold. Melinda shuddered as the finger was withdrawn callously.

'What would you like me to do now?' Sophia asked.

It was another question that completely confounded Melinda. Slaves were not entitled to want anything, their wishes were irrelevant. 'Now, mistress?' She was so perplexed she forgot to add 'Sophia'.

'Yes, tell me. It would amuse me.' She was still standing behind Melinda. She traced a long fingernail, varnished a crimson red, down Melinda's spine.

'I . . . I . . .' Melinda was speechless. It was so long since she had been asked a question of this sort that she found even the word 'I' difficult to pronounce. She knew she had to think of some reply. 'I would like to kiss you, mistress Sophia,' she said, though it wasn't really what she desired. What she wanted more than anything was to watch as Sophia stripped off her clothes, then lay beside her on the bed, their bodies pressed together, squirming against each other, face to face.

'Stand up.'

Melinda obeyed at once.

Sophia unbuttoned her jacket. Under it she wore a three-quarter cup bra in cream lace. Her breasts were large and it thrust them upwards and together to form a cleavage of billowing cushions of deeply tanned flesh.

'You may kiss my breasts,' she said quietly.

Melinda did not hesitate. She turned round and dipped her head, so her lips touched the top of Sophia's left breast. She kissed the right breast too and felt a rush of pleasure.

'The nipples . . .'

They were visible under the lace, erect and each surrounded by a large brown areola. Melinda ran her lips over the lace and kissed them through the material, one then the other. She held her hands behind her back, not daring to touch as well as kiss.

'Harder . . .'

She sucked the cream lace and the nipple into her mouth.

'Use your teeth.'

Melinda caught Sophia's left nipple between her teeth and bit it lightly.

'Harder, girl . . .'

She bit more deeply.

'Harder . . .' Sophia's tone was insistent. Melinda's teeth were almost grinding together. She couldn't believe anyone would want more, but she obeyed, clamping her teeth down on the lace and the puckered flesh it contained.

'Now the other one . . .'

Melinda bit with the same ferocity on the right nipple. Sophia made a low animal-like noise.

'Guard,' she shouted.

The key grated in the lock immediately, as the guard waiting outside opened the door.

'*Si?*'

'Give me your whip,' Sophia said.

The guard took a short, multi-lashed whip from her belt. It had a fat cylindrical handle braided in leather. This time, Sophia did not order the guard to leave.

Melinda was astonished when Sophia handed the whip to her, and then went to stand directly in front of the mirror. She put her hands out to grasp each side of its frame and walked her feet back so she could bend over, pushing her buttocks into the air.

'Push my skirt up,' she ordered.

Melinda pulled the tight skirt up until it was over Sophia's hips. Her heart was sinking. Above all she hoped Sophia was not going to make Melinda use the whip on her. She hated it. Her nature was to be submissive, to *take* punishment, not to *inflict* it.

Sophia's buttocks were full and fleshy. She was wearing French knickers made of the same cream lace as the bra; the details of her body were clearly visible underneath, as was the matching suspender belt that held the flesh-coloured stockings taut on her thighs. At her crotch Melinda could see that her labia were completely hairless, though, judging from the shadows of stubble that surrounded them, not naturally so. Melinda felt another strong pang of desire.

'Good,' Sophia said. She was looking down between her legs. 'I didn't intend this, you know. I just came to look at you. But there's something about you . . .' She raised her head and looked directly into the mirror. For a moment Melinda wondered if someone was watching.

'Use the whip,' Sophia said, her voice husky and deep.

It was what Melinda dreaded. But she had come from Paris with a reputation, through no fault of her own, for disobedience and she certainly did not want to start her relationship with her new Masters on the same note. She raised the whip.

'No,' Sophia said at once. 'The handle, use the handle.' She said it as though Melinda was a total fool for not knowing what she wanted.

But Melinda still did not understand.

'Come on. The handle . . . fuck me with it, girl,' Sophia said, in the same tone.

Her fears dispelled, Melinda felt a surge of excitement. She reversed the whip and gripped the handle awkwardly by the top end where the lashes were threaded into it.

'Do it now.' Sophia was impatient, her bottom wriggling from side to side.

Melinda put one hand on the loose crotch of the French knickers and pulled them aside. In the mirror she could see the guard watching intently, her eyes riveted to Sophia's body. She wished Sophia had ordered the guard to leave again so they could share the intimacy she had felt before, but apparently the feeling was not mutual. Sophia appeared not to mind the mannish guard staring into her exposed sex.

Experimentally, Melinda prodded the end of the handle into Sophia's hairless and rather thin labia, which covered the opening of her vagina.

'Yes,' Sophia encouraged.

Melinda pushed forward and watched the braided leather slide in, the wetness of Sophia's sex easing its passage, the labia closing around it, stretched even thinner by the breadth of its handle.

'Deeper,' Sophia ordered.

Melinda pushed again, half the handle buried now.

'All of it,' Sophia insisted.

Melinda pushed against the base of the handle. With little resistance the broad shaft disappeared into Sophia's sex.

'Fuck me with it.' The crudity did not match her expensive elegance. She was looking into the mirror, her head up, the sinews of her neck strained, her knuckles white as her hands grasped the frame of the mirror.

Melinda pulled the whip handle out then pushed it back in again, all the way in, not wanting to be accused of being too timid. As she pulled it out for the second time she saw the leather handle had been darkened by Sophia's juices. The guard edged forward to get a better view.

'Faster,' Sophia ordered.

Melinda increased the pace, holding the lace of the French knickers aside with one hand as her other manipulated the whip. She felt her own excitement coursing through her body, the desire she had conceived for this woman at fever pitch. She watched keenly as the handle slid to and fro, the lashes of the whip shaking like the branches of a tree in the wind. How she yearned to hold her and kiss her mouth and squirm her body into the lush softness Sophia displayed. Her clitoris seemed to be forcing its way out from under her labia, swelling and pulsating. Her big nipples too seemed to throb.

'Don't stop, don't stop,' Sophia panted, unable to hold her head up any longer. 'When I tell you . . . Just hold it in, hold it deep,' she said, having to drag the words out between the waves of sensation that engulfed her body. She was on the brink of orgasm, every nerve in her body on edge, her muscles locked, tendons stretched. She felt the handle pulled back out once more, and then it started forward, the tough braided leather harsh and abrasive, painful almost. She knew she was ready. 'Now,' she ordered.

Melinda jammed the handle home and held it there. She could see Sophia's labia contracting, her body rigid, every muscle taut. She felt her own clitoris pulse in sympathy. Instinctively, as she saw Sophia relax, as the orgasm escaped her body like a whisper, she let go of the whip. Slowly the dark-haired woman's body squeezed the leather out, expelling it from her sex with infinite slowness until it fell, with a clunk, to the floor. Only then did Sophia straighten up, looking at herself in the mirror steadily and for quite a long time. Again Melinda wondered if anyone had been watching this display.

Calmly she turned back to Melinda. She adjusted the crotch of the French knickers, pulling them back to cover her sex, tightened one of the cream suspenders to iron out a wrinkle that had appeared in one of the stockings, then pulled her skirt down over her thighs. She buttoned up her jacket. Despite the heat of the room and her orgasm, not a single bead of perspiration had broken from her pores. Sweat, on the other hand, ran down Melinda's face and neck, forming a rivulet between her breasts.

'So hot,' Sophia said, running her finger over Melinda's cheek to collect a bead of sweat. She licked it off. 'Do you still want to kiss me?'

'Yes, mistress Sophia.'

Immediately, Sophia leant forward, wrapped a hand around Melinda's neck and kissed her, plunging her tongue into her mouth and squirming her lips against Melinda's.

'Like that?' she asked, when she'd finished.

'Yes, mistress.'

Sophia's hand still held Melinda's neck. 'I love your heat,' she said, moving her hand down over Melinda's shoulder-blades to the small of her back. 'I love your body,' she said as her hand travelled over Melinda's buttocks. 'Open your legs.'

Melinda obeyed at once.

'You are not to come. Do you understand? If you feel yourself getting too close, you must tell me.' She was looking directly into Melinda's green eyes as if trying to find something there. 'Do you understand?'

'Yes, mistress Sophia.'

Sophia's hand rounded Melinda's hip and caressed the top of her thigh.

'Hold her,' she said, addressing the guard.

The guard came up behind Melinda and put her arm around her neck pulling her back against the grey uniform. Sophia's fingers parted Melinda's labia and found her clitoris with ease.

'So swollen,' she said, as she rubbed her finger against it. 'Like a little cock.'

She circled the little nut of nerves with the tip of her fingernail and Melinda felt her body tremble.

Sophia's other hand went to her left nipple, the red fingernails pinching it hard. She knew Melinda's reaction to pain was almost indistinguishable from a wave of pleasure.

'I think I will enjoy having you as my slave. You are very responsive, very pliant. I have many . . .', she thought of the right word, '. . . devices which I like to use on my slaves.' Her finger left Melinda's clitoris and delved deeper, finding her vagina and probing inside. It made a circle, pushing the spongy flesh aside. 'I get such a pleasure from administering pain. And you, I know, get such pleasure from accepting it. Very neat. A circle. Like the one I am making in your cunt.' Again the crudity of language seemed odd coming from Sophia's cultured mouth.

'Oh, mistress.'

'Yes, child?'

But Melinda had no words to express her feelings. Only her body could do that. She felt the waves of pleasure pounding in her nerves and knew she was approaching orgasm.

Sophia's finger went back to Melinda's clitoris, pushing it up and down, as her fingernails relinquished their grip on her left nipple and transferred to the right. Two little crescents remained in the puckered flesh where the nails had been. 'Do you want to come?'

'Oh yes, mistress.'

'Mistress *Sophia*,' she corrected.

'Mistress Sophia.'

'You know you must not?'

'Yes, mistress Sophia.' Sophia's finger was hard, pressing Melinda's clitoris back against her pubic bone and dragging it up and down, as her fingernails pinched her right nipple.

Melinda's body trembled visibly against the guard's hard body. The guard's arm tightened around her neck making it difficult for Melinda to catch her breath. But that only served to increase her excitement.

Sophia saw it all in her eyes, saw how close Melinda was. It was a trial, to see if she would obey, to find out what she was capable of. Relentlessly, she ground her finger into the tiny knot of nerves.

'No, no . . .' Melinda gasped. 'I can't take any more, mistress.'

'No more?' Sophia taunted.

'Please, please, mistress Sophia.' It was against every instinct in her body but she knew she had to obey. That mattered more.

'Very well,' Sophia said. She pulled her hands away from Melinda's body and nodded for the guard to release her. Melinda slumped to the floor, unable to support herself.

'I am pleased. Very pleased. You have performed well. Your submission will be tested many times at our establishment but I think you will be up to it.'

Sophia turned to the mirror, adjusted her clothes and her hair, and strode to the cell door. 'I don't want her touching herself again,' she said to the guard, not looking at Melinda. 'See to it.' And with that she walked elegantly out of the cell, her head held as high as when she'd entered; the leather whip lying on the floor, damp with her juices, was the only sign of what had occurred.

For the first time in her stay at the halfway house Melinda saw the burly guard smile. It was an odd crooked smile and revealed three broken teeth. She stooped to pick the whip off the floor, sniffing it appreciatively before putting it back in her belt.

Reaching into her pocket she extracted a black nylon stocking. She stretched it out between her hands, reducing it to a thin, tight cord, then caught hold of Melinda's arms, one by one, and expertly trussed them behind her back with the nylon, knotting the stocking together tightly just above the elbows, forcing them together, pulling Melinda's shoulders back and consequently thrusting her breasts out. Almost before Melinda knew what had happened the cell door had been slammed shut and she heard the key turning in its lock.

She looked at herself in the mirror. Her body was still throbbing, still aching for the release it would not achieve. The bondage was simple but extremely effective. The material cut deeply into her flesh. There was no way she could reach her sex but she could strain her hands forward to cup her breasts. It would not make her come but the feeling was comforting. She struggled to her feet with difficulty, then stood pressing her thighs together, trying to bring pressure to bear on her clitoris. She desperately wanted to come, while the cell was still scented with Sophia's perfume and the aroma of her sex, while she could still feel Sophia's mouth against hers and her finger in her body, while the image of Sophia's labia enveloping the handle of the whip was still fresh in her mind.

In the mirror, viewed from the front, her hands looked disembodied, the rest of the arm hidden from view. They were reddened by the bondage, the veins standing out as they squeezed her tits. Her body was still covered in sweat.

Was this direct disobedience? Sophia had ordered her not to come, but that was when she was with her, touching her, provoking her. Left alone, was she not returned to the limbo of the halfway house, delivery not yet complete? She didn't know. But that was how she justified it to herself. Sophia had stirred her body beyond endurance. Melinda squeezed her clitoris rhythmically between her thighs as her fingers pinched at her nipples. Great surges of feeling pulsed through her body, the peculiar bondage fuelling her passion. She could feel the wetness of her labia escaping her thighs as she saw the crystal clear image of Sophia's exquisite body bending over the mirror, the whip sticking up from her loins like some exotic mushroom. She stared at her eyes in the mirror and saw the excitement dancing in them.

She was close. The pressure from her thighs pressed in on her clitoris from both sides, pushing it up against the little hood of the labia. She was going to come ...

The key turned in the lock and Melinda froze. The cell door swung open. The guard looked at her long and hard but apparently detected no sign of anything untoward. She dropped a heavy leather harness on the floor, then picked up the discarded black panties. Indicating for Melinda to step into them, the guard pulled them up over Melinda's hips and tightly on to her waist. In her fevered condition the crotch of the panties being forced between her legs made Melinda shudder. Thankfully, as the guard would have been sure to notice and report to Sophia, the touch was not enough to bring her off. The release she had been made to crave so desperately was still denied her.

The guard picked up part of the harness and began wrapping a sheath of thick leather around Melinda's calf. It enclosed the whole of her leg from below the knee to just above the ankle and was secured by means of three small buckles along its length. A chain was attached to a ring sown into the leather just above the Achilles tendon, but its purpose remained unclear.

By means of a pocket knife the guard cut through the nylon stocking that bound Melinda's elbows, the knots too tight to unravel by hand. She went back to the remaining part of the harness and picked it up. There were two long leather cuffs, very like the one on Melinda's calf, but joined together by metal rings. She fitted them over Melinda's lower arms and buckled them tight, effectively binding her arms together in front of her.

Pulling her arms up above her head, the guard slipped the sturdy metal ring that held the cuffs together at the wrists into the metal hook on the chain that hung from the beam in the ceiling. Then she picked up the chain secured to the leg sheath at the ankle, and pulled Melinda's leg back until it was twisted up behind her, and slipped the appropriate link over the hook, holding the leg in position, Melinda's foot at waist height behind her.

The guard smiled her crooked smile and left, locking the door behind her.

Sophia's wishes had been carried out to the letter. Not only could she not touch herself now, in this position it was impossible for her to put any pressure on her clitoris with her thighs, let alone touch her breasts. She had no way now to quell her body's needs. And there was worse. Her position was excruciatingly uncomfortable, her bondage extreme. But the pain of bondage had always been twisted by her body into a throbbing, overwhelming sensation of pleasure. What made it more acute was being able to see herself so clearly in the mirror; the way her sex was covered by the tight black panties, how her wetness had sucked the material up to outline the furrow of her labia, how her breasts were stretched by the position of her arms. She looked like a dancer locked in an endless pirouette.

The image that stared back at her from the mirror was perfect. Bondage was the symbol of her submission. It was the ultimate subjugation, she was giving up even the power to move, as she gave up everything else. Was that why seeing herself in the tight leather and taut chains thrilled her so much? Submission was, after all, what she wanted. It was what moved her most profoundly; the impulse, she had discovered, that ruled her life.

As the cramp in her muscles increased and the pain was transformed by her already overheated body into waves of a peculiar warped pleasure, every nerve she possessed screamed for a release that would never come. And it was a vicious circle. Melinda's pleasure came in denial as much as in gratification, as it would for any true slave. The more she was denied, the more impossible it was to achieve fulfilment. The more her temperature rose, the hotter her passion, the greater her need; and therefore, the circle complete, the more there was to be denied.

She tried to shut her eyes, to shield herself from the image in the mirror. But that proved useless. Her mind merely threw the image of the frozen pirouette on to a screen in her head, and played it over and over again.

There was no escape. Pleasure became tortured pain, and pain teasing pleasure. She was trapped on the brink of orgasm, able to look down into the precipice but quite unable to throw herself over it, poised cunningly between the gates of heaven and the doors of hell.

Two

The man regarded her with little interest. He was short and sturdy with dark hair, a Mediterranean complexion, his skin tanned to leather from years of exposure to the sun. He was wearing the same grey uniform as the female guard.

He was too short to reach the metal hook from which Melinda was suspended, so he pulled the wooden bed over and stood on it, releasing the chain to her ankle first and then unhooking the ring that held her wrists.

Melinda slumped to the floor, her aching muscles unable to support her weight. The blood flowed back into the veins that had been trapped, making her moan with agony. The man took no notice. He pulled a leather gag from his pocket, a large black rubber ball attached to a thick leather strap, came up behind Melinda and stuffed the ball into her mouth, buckling the strap tightly behind her neck. The rubber ball filled her mouth, pressing down on her tongue and stretching her lips at the corners of her mouth. He also pulled out a leather blindfold – a piece of mask-shaped leather, cut to fit over the nose and around the sockets of the eye, and padded on the inside so as to exclude all light. This too was strapped tightly around the back of Melinda's head with equal callousness. She was plunged into the anonymity of darkness.

Her release and this treatment could mean only one thing. Sophia had come to inspect her and now she was being taken to her new Master, to Sophia's home and her husband. Judging by the way Sophia had already treated her, it was a prospect that made Melinda tingle with anticipation. The desire she had felt for Sophia and the fact that she would undoubtedly be intimate with her again, alone or with her husband, thrilled her. But more than that, there was the prospect of a new Master. What would he be like? Would he be as attractive as his wife or as imaginative? What would he want to do to her or make her do? And what of their household? How many slaves and how were they organised? Every establishment she had been in so far had been completely different, apart from the two basic rules. What would this new one have in store for her? So many questions crowded into Melinda's mind in the darkness and she now knew they would soon be answered.

The male guard was unstrapping the leather sheath from her calf. As soon as it was free he turned his attention to the metal rings that held the long leather cuffs on Melinda's arms together. There were three in all; one at the bottom by the wrists, one in the middle and a third just under the elbow. They were held by a small clip, which the guard quickly unlatched.

Pulling Melinda by one arm, he indicated that he wanted her to stand. As soon as she was on her feet he twisted her arms behind her back and fastened the metal rings back into the clips, binding her arms securely in this position, her shoulders yanked back, her breasts thrust forward.

Melinda felt a collar being wound around her neck and buckled into place. Attached to it was a metal chain that swung from side to side, grazing her breasts until it eventually settled between them. It was cold and made her already hard nipples even stiffer.

Without a word, the guard took the chain and pulled her forward by it. She felt the slightly cooler air in the corridor and counted the number of steps to the small bathroom so she knew when they had passed it. She heard another door being unlocked with a grinding of metal and she was hauled through it, though the stone floor underfoot felt the same.

'*Scarpe*,' he said, bringing her to a halt after a dozen steps. She had no idea what he meant. '*Scarpe*,' he repeated angrily, not wanting any delay. He dropped the chain, and it grazed her breasts again. '*Scarpe*.' This time he got to his knees and lifted her foot, almost making her overbalance as he pushed it into a black high-heeled shoe. Wanting to co-operate, she searched with her other foot until she found the second high heel and slipped into it.

She felt him tugging on the chain again and walked forwards, tottering at first, not having worn such high shoes for some time. She suddenly had an image of herself, seeing herself as a stranger would view her – the perfect slave, hands bound behind her, breasts thrust out, the gag and blindfold drawn tightly across her face, high heels hardening the muscles of her legs, the smooth black panties her only covering – being led forward docilely to her fate. She had no will, no emotion. She was reduced to an object on the end of a chain, a commodity to be bought and sold like any other piece of merchandise.

The image thrilled her so much that a shudder of the most profound pleasure raked through her nerves. It was, after all, everything she had ever wanted.

As the guard opened the exterior door Melinda felt

a rush of warm air invade the comparative cool of the corridor. She was pulled outside, then brought to a halt. The chain dropped between her breasts again.

She felt the hot sun on her near-naked body. How long Sophia had ordered her to be held in bondage she had no way of knowing. She had imagined it was now late afternoon whereas, in fact, going by the heat of the sun, it was still only just after lunch. She listened intently, in order to find out what was going on. She heard two men's voices talking in Italian and then that of a woman, who Melinda recognised as the burly guard. Though she couldn't understand a word of what was being said, it was obvious they were talking about her in derogatory terms, and they seemed in no particular hurry to take her wherever she was meant to be going.

She heard the noise of an engine, the distinctive sound of a diesel engine being started and then being put into reverse. She smelt acrid exhaust fumes and heard the tinny sound of a panelled van door being opened.

It was at that moment pandemonium broke loose. A car, a big powerful car by the sound of it, skidded to a halt in a shower of dirt and gravel. Four men jumped from it almost before it had come to rest; big muscular men carrying wooden pickaxe handles. The man nearest to the driver of the van opened the van door and hauled him out. The driver did not care to stand and fight and ran off as fast as he could. The guard who had brought Melinda out from her cell did not fight either and raced away, chasing on the heels of the first guard.

The halfway house was situated at the bottom of a track in a secluded and very woody area. It did not take long for the two guards to disappear into the trees. The men did not pursue them. There was no need.

The female guard was more problematic. She squared up to the first man who approached her and, as he lunged forward to try and grab her, kicked him in the chin so hard that he crashed to the ground. He was only saved from another vicious blow to his crotch by a fourth man, who body-charged her. She didn't stay down, however. She scrambled up to her knees, caught the other man's legs with her arms and toppled him to the ground, immediately attacking him with her fists and battering his face and chest.

The man she had kicked managed to overcome the pain and rolled over to try and grab her arms. But as soon as she felt his hands clawing at her she wrenched her arms away and turned her attention to him, hammer blows flying into his face, one landing squarely on his nose and causing blood to flow from both nostrils.

Melinda, of course, could see nothing of this. She'd heard the scuffle of feet on the sandy track and the cries of pain and exasperation as the two men tried to subdue the battling female guard. She knew something was wrong but could not imagine what. She heard a man running towards her and the next thing she knew he was behind her and she was literally swept off her feet. He hoisted her into his arms as easily as if she were a baby and carried her at a trot to the car, where he threw her on to the back seat and then climbed in after her.

Immediately he was inside he shouted to the others in Italian. The man who had chased off the driver had disappeared inside the halfway house, where he had torn out the telephone line to delay word of what had happened getting to the OIM. Similarly, he had opened the bonnet of the van and ripped out the distributor system and all its wiring. This task complete, he climbed behind the wheel of the car where he revved the engine and tooted the horn for the other two men to join them, laughing as he watched them fight.

It was not as easy for them, however. The female guard fought like a tiger, clawing and ripping at their clothes, punching and kicking any part of their anatomy she could reach. Her hand had caught the front of a shirt and torn every button off, while she had only just failed to smack a vicious upper-cut into one of the men's balls. She had grabbed a clump of hair and tried to pull its owner over by it, making him scream in pain as he desperately tried to pry her fingers away. With both hands trying to remove her fingers from his hair, he had left himself vulnerable; she pulled him forward on to a short jab that hit him in the right eye and another punch that landed square on his chin, making his head reel.

The man whose nose was bleeding profusely over all three of them managed to grasp the pickaxe handle he had dropped at the start of the struggle, and he delivered a swift blow with it to the woman's skull. It was enough to free her fingers from his companion's hair and allow them both to scramble to their feet. One made it to the car safely but the other man was caught by the ankles as the woman recovered. He was three steps from the car, and dragged her behind him until he could pull himself, by grabbing the open door, into the front seat. The driver started the car forward immediately but still the woman hung on to one of the man's ankles. She even managed to heave herself forward and bite it before the speed of the car and the gravel track took their toll and she finally had to relinquish her grip.

Not that she was finished. With remarkable physical stamina the female guard hauled herself to her feet, pulled up one of the rocks that bordered the track at intervals of two or three feet, and threw it at the car. It sailed in a parabolic arc and, as the car followed a bend in the drive, landed plumb in the middle of the bonnet, leaving a huge crater in the thin metal, though not, apparently, having enough force to affect the mechanics.

Melinda heard the crash and started, expecting the car to grind to a halt. Instead, the track turned into a tarmac road and the car accelerated. It slowed again after a couple of minutes and turned left, its speed picking up considerably as it obviously headed down a main road.

The men in the car exchanged exclamations of disgust in Italian. It did not take a grasp of the language to understand their tone, or the obscenities they were obviously directing at the woman who had put up such stubborn resistance. The man sitting on Melinda's right was trying to staunch his nosebleed, while the one in the front seat had lost a handful of hair and had a black eye that had swollen more than half his face. The amusement and laughter of the other two men – who had not been involved in the fracas – was not appreciated.

Melinda had been squeezed between the men on the back seat, her position made more uncomfortable by the fact her arms were still bound behind her. It had all happened so suddenly and so unexpectedly that she had hardly had time to react. She had no idea what was going on. It was obvious that the attack was aimed at her, its purpose to kidnap her from the halfway house. The men had waited – for hours or days, she had no way of knowing – until she had emerged to be transferred to the van for her journey to the new Master. Though her heart was beating so fast, it made her feel dizzy; strangely, she felt absolutely no fear.

Gradually the sound of the voices returned to normal and the men eventually lapsed into silence. The car appeared to be driving at a fairly consistent speed along winding roads, the momentum swaying their bodies from side to side on each bend.

As far as she could tell the men seemed to be paying little attention to her semi-naked body. Perhaps they were looking at her but they certainly made no attempt to touch her and no conversation which concerned her developed. Because of this, her first thought as to the motive for her kidnapping was that it was, despite the obvious commotion she had heard, an elaborate charade organised by the OIM. For what purpose and to what end she could only speculate; perhaps it was intended as a way to shake her up emotionally, to make her more fearful and more pliant.

But even if this was not the case, even if she was genuinely being kidnapped by this gang of ruffians, it was excitement, not fear, that dominated Melinda's emotions. Perhaps she would have felt differently if the men in the car had stopped and taken her into a clearing somewhere and raped her one by one. But they had not, and some sixth sense told Melinda that this was not their intention. They were still showing little interest in her. She was a commodity, a chattel they had stolen under very specific orders, and it was quite clear they were not allowed to damage the goods.

That degree of obedience, she reasoned, came from a special source. It was the sort of discipline she had seen over and over again in the staff employed by the Masters she had served. Whoever had gone to all this trouble to abduct her had done so for very special reasons, which did not include doing her any harm.

The more she thought about it, the more she realised the operation must have been planned by someone who knew the ways of the OIM, someone who knew about the halfway houses and the transference of slaves from one Master to another. The four men had not been casually passing by when they decided to kidnap a beautiful, bound and semi-naked girl – that *would* be frightening. They had to know where to go and had waited until Melinda was brought out into the open, the point at which the guards were most vulnerable to attack. Whoever planned the operation knew exactly how the organisation was run, down to the fact that the girls were always transferred by van. It was either some sort of trick conceived by the OIM or a plot devised by someone who had been intimately connected with it.

The car seemed to be slowing up, as it wound its way along more zigzagging corners with ever-steeper gradients. Occasionally the men would chatter in Italian – usually, Melinda thought, to rag the two men about being so badly mauled by the female guard – but mostly the journey was passed in silence.

The one thing Melinda could not work out was whether the kidnapping had been specifically intended to net *her* or whether it was planned to take whoever happened to be the slave due for transfer on the day. At first she'd assumed they were after her, but she realised that all the halfway houses had more than one slave at any one time, different slaves being distributed to different Masters, some on the way in and others out. The car may simply have been waiting for the first one to emerge and had snatched whoever it happened to be.

On the other hand, they might have been waiting especially for Melinda. Whoever was behind all this could well have had access to the video link used to sell and barter slaves between Masters, and may have seen the special viewing that had been transmitted from Paris as the Countess, Melinda's last Master, had sought a buyer for her. They had then decided, unilaterally, that they didn't want to wait the customary three months until she was available again and had arranged a short cut. As she thought more and more about it, it was this scenario that made most sense to Melinda and most excited her. One of the Masters had taken matters into his own hands, bypassing the normal procedures.

It excited her because to be desired that much by a Master was the ultimate goal for any slave. For much of the time, slaves had to pray for their Master's attention, hope against hope that they would be called to his presence, called to spend time with him, even if that meant being punished for his pleasure. What Melinda craved, like all the slaves, was contact of any sort with the man – or in the Countess's case, the woman – who dominated their lives.

To be taken like this implied a special interest and desire. It meant that the Master had spent time planning and ordering events. It implied he wanted her badly. As much as Sophia had excited her, as much as Melinda had looked forward to being her slave and to meeting her husband, this new and totally unexpected development had set her pulse racing. Almost unconsciously she felt herself wriggling against the leather seat of the car, unable to contain her arousal.

'*Pute*,' one of the men sitting next to her said. He addressed a long sentence to his companions, who turned and looked at Melinda. It was obvious he had noticed her condition and had commented on it to his colleagues.

'Hot little bitch,' the man in the front seat said in broken English. 'Are you?' he asked.

Melinda nodded, seeing no reason to deny it.

For the first time, she felt – though she had no way of knowing whether it was true – that the men were looking at her with more than a casual interest. She felt the man next to her moving his arm, as if to touch her breast.

'Paolo!' a voice shouted quickly, which was then followed by a string of Italian words in rebuke. Melinda was not to be touched, not in that way at least.

Melinda tried to control her feelings, not wanting to provoke another outburst by drawing attention to herself or, worse, risk them deciding that whatever orders they had been given could be stretched a little to include a prolonged interlude in some secluded spot.

The car seemed to have climbed up a fairly steep hillside and was descending now, still swinging from side to side as it took winding corners. Melinda had not heard another car or lorry come along the road in either direction for some time. It was obviously not well-used.

Another thirty minutes passed, with no sign of traffic, before the car slowed and turned right, then began driving over what was clearly no more than a rough track. It wallowed in deep potholes and leapt into the air on steep bumps, while the tyres protested constantly, spraying out stones and sand as they tried to maintain their grip on the ground. After ten or fifteen minutes of this bone-jarring ride, the car came to a halt.

Melinda heard all four doors open and the men got out, leaving her alone in the back seat, able for the first time to ease forward and relieve her aching arm and shoulder muscles. They left the doors open and she heard them greeting at least one other man. They stretched their legs and lit cigarettes as they talked, apparently casually. As she listened, she heard another, less familiar sound. At first she couldn't identify it but then she realised it was the sound of nearby horses snorting and snuffling against their bits as they stood waiting.

The tone of the men's voices changed. It was time to get on. The cigarettes were stubbed out and Melinda was dragged from the interior of the car by hard, calloused hands. She felt one of the men unstrapping the leather blindfold; suddenly she experienced a searing pain as sunlight hit her eyes after such a long time in the dark. She screwed her eyes up tight and waited for them to adjust, tears escaping from under her eyelids.

They pulled her over to the horses. She could feel their warmth and smell their pleasant animal odour, though she did not dare open her eyes yet. One of the men was unclipping the leather harness on her arms and, as soon as they were free, another flood of pain hit her as her shoulders, cramped for so long, went into spasm. The leather tubes were unbuckled, leaving her arms completely free.

Tentatively, Melinda opened her eyes, squinting through her eyelids to see. She was standing on a grassy hillside which led into a beautiful wooded valley. There were no houses and she could see that the track they had travelled down was no more than a gravel path across the grass. Three chestnut mares stood together patiently, their bridles tied to the trunk of a nearby tree.

She looked round to see the four men who had been responsible for the kidnapping climbing back into the car, a black saloon of a make she didn't recognise. In a cloud of dust kicked up from the tyres, the car reversed, then sped off down the track. It soon disappeared from view.

Melinda had been left with two men. They were both powerfully built, but it was their outfits that most puzzled Melinda. They were wearing white tunics, belted at the waist and extending down to their knees, their hems cut into a square pattern like a child's drawing of castellated battlements. Their legs and arms were bare and they wore leather sandals on their feet. She had only ever seen clothes like this in films set in ancient Rome. Why they were so bizarrely dressed she had no idea.

The man who had unfastened her harness now removed her gag, pulling it out of her mouth with a plop. He was almost entirely bald, his head polished and shining in what was now the late afternoon sun. Having the rubber ball forced into her mouth for such a long period of time had made Melinda incredibly thirsty. They had apparently anticipated this and the man handed her a peculiar water bottle, made from what looked like animal skin, that had been hanging around his neck. She drank eagerly.

'This off,' he said, as soon as she'd finished the water, snapping the elasticated waist of the black panties to indicate his intentions.

Melinda wriggled the panties down her legs. The bald man watched her with more than casual interest, his eyes examining the light fleece of her pubis and the beginning of the labia below it. His companion, who also inspected Melinda critically, began untying the horses. Handing the reins to the bald man, he came up behind Melinda and, with little effort at all, hoisted her over the leather saddle on the horse so she was lying over it on her stomach. Taking a rope, he quickly wrapped it a couple of times around Melinda's wrists, then threaded it under the belly of the horse and secured it around her ankles, effectively tying her to the horse. The two men mounted their horses and, leading hers behind them, set off down towards the valley.

Melinda could see very little. It was too much of an effort to raise her head and look up so she contented herself with watching the well-worn but narrow track pass under the horse's hooves. The sun was still hot, and she felt it burning into her back and her naked buttocks. Her position on the horse was not uncomfortable, certainly in comparison to the ride in the car. It was a relief only to be bound lightly, especially in a way that put no new pressure on her shoulders, which still ached not only from the car journey but also from her bondage in the cell earlier that morning.

It did not take long to reach the heavily wooded valley, though the horses never reached more than a walking pace. Melinda noticed that the path changed from rough gravel to sections of paving-stones interspersed with grass as they passed through a dense stand of trees, the shade of which brought a chill to the air. Soon the grass disappeared altogether and they were travelling on a wide path entirely paved with very white stones. She strained her head upwards to see that they had reached a large clearing surrounded on all sides by evergreen trees. In front of them was a stone wall, set in the middle of which were two wooden gates, one of which, she could see, was being opened as they approached. The man on the gates also wore a white Roman tunic.

They passed through the gates into a courtyard paved in the white stone that had been used for the path. The horses were brought to a halt and Melinda heard the two men dismount. The rope around Melinda's wrists and ankles was untied and she was hauled off the horse.

The building that faced her was, like the men's costumes, straight out of a Hollywood film set in ancient Rome. It was a perfect reproduction of a Roman villa, a two-storey building with triangular gables supporting the roof and decorative white stone columns at regular intervals around the outside walls. A shallow trough of water made from stone surrounded the whole structure. It was large, the sort of house that would have been owned by a Roman senator, a man of substance and power.

The courtyard that surrounded it was also large, and Melinda could see several women tending the flower-beds and shrubbery that had been landscaped into the area. It was clear to Melinda that they were slaves, as most of them were naked and obviously being watched by overseers, men and women in the white Roman tunics. All the Masters' establishments she had ever been in had used slaves for work in the gardens and in the house, as well as for more intimate duties. In some households, the working slaves and the slaves that served the Master directly were kept quite separate; in others, they performed both roles. Melinda had no way of knowing which applied here, but it was quite obvious that the Master of this villa was quite familiar with the OIM.

The slaves all worked in little gangs of three or four and Melinda counted twelve in all, with no sign of any male slaves. The females who were not naked wore complicated leather harnesses around their breasts and loins which, Melinda knew from previous experience, were used as a form of punishment, inflicting discomfort while the slave was put to work. The overseers carried short leather straps, split in two at one end, which were more than occasionally brought to bear on the rumps of slacking workers.

The bald-headed man took Melinda by the wrist. Immediately in front of a short flight of white marble steps that led up to the main entrance of the building was a cylindrical stone column, which was as broad as a very large tree and at least ten feet tall. At the back of the column, at well over head height, a metal ring was set and, attached to it, were two thick chains. There was a similar ring and chains immediately underneath the first but almost at ground level.

The bald overseer stood Melinda in front of the column, facing the house. She saw four metal manacles lying on the ground, which the overseer picked up and snapped over her wrists and ankles; the manacle hinged on one side and locked on the other, the lock apparently having some sort of built-in combination, therefore not, Melinda imagined, a genuine Roman artefact.

Satisfied that the manacles were correctly secured, the overseer reached around the column for the chains, starting with the ones on top. The manacles had a clip on the outside into which he fitted a link of the chain, arranging the length so Melinda's arms were forced up above her head and back around the column. Getting to his knees, he clipped the lower chains in place in a similar manner, stretching

Melinda's legs open and back. Not only was she spread-eagled against the column but her torso was thrust out, her breasts and pubic bone most prominent.

Once the job was completed, the bald man walked back to his companion without a second glance. Although, bound as she was, Melinda could not turn her head to see, she heard the horses being led away, their hooves echoing on the white paving-stones. They finally came into her field of vision as they were walked past the left-hand corner of the house and into what must have been – since their hooves continued to echo – another courtyard beyond.

Almost as soon as the noise had died away, a short plump woman in what by now was the familiar Roman tunic, emerged through the columns that formed the entrance to the house. She was carrying a wooden box in one hand and a small metal anvil in the other. As soon as she reached the stone column, she dropped to her knees and set the anvil and box in front of her. A gold chain was extracted from the box. It was set with what appeared to be a sapphire, though Melinda could not believe such a large stone could be real.

The woman pushed the manacle on Melinda's right wrist down as far as it would go on to her foot, then wound the chain around her ankle to measure it. Skilfully, and with practised ease, she used a small hammer and cold chisel to strike four or five links off the chain. With equal precision, she closed it around Melinda's ankle, rested the anvil close against Melinda's foot, opened a link, threaded the link at the other end into it and hammered the open link closed, thus sealing the gold chain in place. All this was the work of seconds and almost before Melinda knew what had happened, the woman had gone.

A heavy silence fell, interrupted only occasionally by the sound of the strap being applied to one of the errant slaves, and sometimes a yelp in response. The position Melinda had been left in was extremely uncomfortable. Not only did the iron manacles bite into her wrists and ankles, but the way her arms and legs were forced backwards put renewed pressure on her shoulders and made her buttocks ache.

But despite the pain, in fact precisely *because* of it, Melinda felt her body humming like a radio, her excitement like a transmitter sending signals to her nerves. Her big knob-like nipples were stiff, her labia parted by the position of her legs. She was displayed, pinned down like a butterfly, an exhibit for anyone and everyone to see.

It had all happened so quickly; one minute she was on her way to Sophia and the next she'd been whisked away to what was, with one or two obvious concessions to the twentieth century, ancient Rome. Whatever awaited her in his strange villa, whoever was responsible for her abduction, clearly had definite plans for her and she could not help but be impatient to find out what they were.

She examined the house carefully as a way of trying to forget the state of her aching body and her over-aroused nerves. Though the style was, as far as she could tell, authentically Roman, many modern conveniences had been incorporated into the structure. The windows were all glazed and she could see electric light fittings concealed in the flower-beds and around the shallow ponds. She couldn't see anyone in the house looking out, however, though occasionally she saw movement as someone hurried about their work. But that didn't mean she wasn't being watched. She thought, though she could not be sure, that she saw the lens of a video camera poking out from under the eave of the roof. She even thought she saw it move, focusing, perhaps, on her.

She heard footsteps on the paving behind her and voices speaking in English, both female. Two women passed the column on their way into the house. One, a striking but petite redhead, stopped and looked back.

'She's new . . .' she said, stopping her companion by touching her arm.

Her companion was blonde, her hair long and flowing. Both women were slim and both wore brightly coloured silk togas, belted at the waist by a heavy gold chain.

The blonde turned and looked critically at Melinda.

'Mmm, nice eyes.'

The redhead came to stand at Melinda's side. 'Nice body.' Her hand touched Melinda's nipple, making her shudder.

'Come on, Dee. I'm hungry.'

'Don't you want to play with her?'

'Maybe later.'

'We might not get a chance later. Once he's taken her, he doesn't like to share.'

'Sometimes he does.'

'Not with the likes of you and I. Only special guests.'

The redhead was stroking Melinda's breasts. 'I'd love to be tied up like that, wouldn't you?'

'God no, what an idea.'

'Oh, I would. So open. So exposed. I mean, look at her. We could do anything to her, anything . . .'

Melinda shuddered again, this time provoked by what the woman was saying.

'See. Did you see that?'

Her hand dropped to the fleece of Melinda's pubis. She caressed the hair gently.

'Come on, Dee.'

'All right, all right . . .' The woman turned and looked at Melinda directly. 'He's never going to let you go. You're too pretty,' she said, before walking away.

Silence quickly returned. Melinda thought about what the women had said. Clearly they were neither slaves nor overseers, nor, from the way they talked, part of the Master's family. They were obviously guests, invited to the villa to enjoy its facilities and perhaps help to entertain its Master.

No one else appeared. Melinda concentrated on what she thought was the camera. She aimed herself at it, holding her breasts out proudly, angling herself towards it as far as the chains permitted, hoping that the Master, whoever he was, had turned on the camera and was watching her. She wanted to show him she was ready, that she was not scared or put off by her experience, that she was up to the challenge he had initiated.

But if he did see her, he gave no sign.

As the sun set and long shadows were cast across the courtyard, Melinda heard the work parties being taken away. They did not come through the front, however, and she caught a glimpse of them only as they walked around the side of the building. They walked in single file, under the close supervision of the two male and two female overseers.

Though it was not cold, the shadows brought a chill to the courtyard which, after the heat of the day, Melinda felt strongly. She began to think she was going to be left outside all night. It would not surprise her. Many of the Masters indulged in a sort of softening-up process, an initiation rite to make sure their slaves appreciated their duties and obligations and were reminded that they had no rights. It was another indication to Melinda that the Master of the villa was more than just familiar with OIM methods.

It was almost dark now and several lights – electric, Melinda guessed, by their power – had come on all over the villa. Lights soon illuminated the courtyard, too, lighting the colourful flowers and shrubs and the water that surrounded the house.

It was then Melinda heard the front door open. A woman strode out, heading straight for Melinda and the stone column, a white rope in her hand.

The rope looked particularly white in contrast to the hand that held it. The woman's skin was not brown, or even dark brown, but black as ebony. Her hair was jet black, too, and cut to within a half an inch of her scalp; so curly that, despite its cropped nature, it still tried to form tiny rings. She was big, too – at least six feet tall – and had muscles that looked as though she worked them hard and regularly. Her arms and thighs were particularly well defined, cords of muscles standing out as though modelled on some anatomical chart. Around her body she wore a swathe of material to cover her small breasts and another was wrapped around her hips. The fabric was a deep saffron colour.

'You hurt?' she asked, her voice as dark and rich as the colour of her skin.

'Yes, mistress.'

The Nubian took Melinda's cheeks and squeezed them between her finger and thumb, turning Melinda's head this way and that, examining her face from one side and then the other.

'The men, they touch you?'

'No, mistress.'

Quickly the Nubian freed the manacles from the chains at Melinda's ankles, allowing her to ease her legs forward.

'I, Bandu,' she said. 'You obey. You know you obey?'

'Yes, mistress.'

'I have to punish if you not obey.'

Bandu's eyes were a brown so dark they were almost black.

They were looking at Melinda intently.

'I punish hard,' she said and, from her physique, Melinda was sure it was true. A whipping from this woman would be hard to forget.

As she reached up to free the chains on her wrists, Bandu's body pressed against Melinda's. It felt as hard as steel. Melinda gasped as she lowered her arms and her shoulders came back to life. As she recovered, Bandu unlocked the manacles and dropped them back on to the ground in front of the column where they had come from.

The Nubian tied the rope around Melinda's waist in such a way as to leave a lead of three or four feet, then she pulled her forward by it. They did not go through the front of the house but around to the side where Melinda had seen the other slaves being taken.

As they rounded the side wall of the villa, Melinda saw that the courtyard closed in to become an almost perfect square; it was surrounded on three sides by outbuildings and on the other by the back wall of the main house. About a third of this space was given over to a huge swimming pool, beautifully tiled in blue mosaics, with stone benches all around it at regular intervals set on delicate white mosaics which covered the surrounds. One wall of the villa was completely open to the water. Melinda could see several men and women dressed in tunics and togas, who were sitting around drinking from elaborate bejewelled gold chalices, or swimming languidly, their bodies naked. The pool was lit from below and water droplets sparkled like tiny prisms as the swimmers created splashes here and there.

Nobody appeared to pay any attention to the naked slave being led by the tall Nubian across the white paved courtyard.

The outbuildings surrounding the central atrium were all of the same height, a single storey, with the same angle on their gabled roofs as the main villa, but they obviously served different purposes. Melinda could see stables built into one and a long row of narrow doors side by side on another; this was obviously, she thought, where the working slaves were housed. They entered an annexe directly attached to the side of the villa, with only one door. Bandu opened the door and led Melinda inside. She found herself in a large rectangular room with a terracotta tiled floor and white plastered walls. Dug into the centre of the floor, like a miniature swimming pool, was a rectangular tank, with stone steps leading down into it, a perfect replica of a Roman bath.

The room was lit by massive candles almost a foot in diameter and mounted on cast-iron stands placed regularly along the walls. Whether from these or something else, the room was filled with a musky incense-like aroma which made Melinda feel a little intoxicated as she breathed it in.

Standing in three corners of the deep bath were three more Nubians. They were, like Bandu, tall, black, with muscular bodies and short-cropped hair, their small breasts half-covered by the water in the bath.

Bandu led Melinda over to the bath, then slipped the rope from her waist. She unwrapped the two swathes of material from her body and stood naked. Her breasts were no more than pockets of flesh on top of the broad cage of her ribs but, against the blackness of her skin, her nipples seemed almost pink. Below, her belly was flat and defined by muscle. Her pubic hair was as short as the hair on her head and just as curly. It was incredibly thick but did not extend on to her labia. Melinda could see the first inch of Bandu's thick lips pressed together tightly, and the dark slit this formed.

'Get on your knees,' Bandu said.

Melinda obeyed at once.

'Lick it for me.' There was no need to specify what 'it' was. Bandu's hand was already drawing Melinda's face to her crotch. Melinda felt the coarse pubic hair against her lips. It was like wire wool. She pushed her tongue now between the black labia and found Bandu's clitoris. To her surprise, it was wet. She tapped it with the tip of her tongue, then pushed it from side to side. Bandu's hand increased its pressure on the back of her head, forcing Melinda, in turn, to press harder.

'Good,' she said. She released her grip, and turned round, bending at the waist and opening her legs wide, the palms of her hands flat on the floor in front of her. 'Do again,' she said.

Melinda stared into the yawning gap of Bandu's sex, its scarlets, reds and pinks like a wound in contrast to the sheen of black flesh that surrounded it. She leant forward and tongued the whole length of it, from her clitoris to the puckered crater of her anus.

She could see the other Nubians watching intently. After three or four long strokes she centred her tongue on Bandu's vagina and pushed up into it as far as the tendons of her tongue would allow.

Bandu's body tensed. Melinda could feel her labia contract, and felt her pushing back against the tongue that invaded her. 'Clit,' she groaned.

Melinda obeyed immediately, tapping at her clitoris again. This time she felt Bandu's body tremble. After only a few seconds she let out a tiny mewing sound. She straightened up, turned and looked into Melinda's eyes.

'Good,' she repeated. She pulled Melinda to her feet by taking her hand and led her down the stone steps into the bath. The water was warm and soapy and Melinda felt a delicious sensation as it enveloped her. She could not stop herself moaning with pleasure.

As Bandu pulled Melinda to the centre of the tank, the other Nubians waded towards her. Each carried a bar of beige-coloured soap that smelt of honey. They began to rub the soap over her body, covering every ounce of flesh, paying special attention, or so it seemed, to her breasts and thighs and buttocks, rubbing the soap between her legs. Fingers kneaded and pummelled her flesh, hands were everywhere.

She felt them spreading her thighs apart and she sensed something hard and slippery being forced against the mouth of her sex. Suddenly it was inside her and she shuddered with sensation. They closed her legs again.

Taking big, natural sponges, the Nubians washed the soap away. Then they pressed themselves into her, all four of them linking arms around her, squashing their hard muscles into her, squeezing her between them. Melinda felt a surge of pleasure at so much human contact, the warm sweet-smelling soapy water adding another dimension, the object inserted in her sex defining the centre of her being.

Slowly they led her up the stone steps and out of the water. There was a big stack of white towels at the side of the tank, and each of the black women took one and began rubbing Melinda dry with it, dividing her body into sections, above and below the waist, back and front.

Melinda felt her body respond. After so little human contact, so much attention was almost overwhelming. She felt how carefully they dried her, lovingly almost, using the towels to caress her, paying special attention to her breasts and buttocks and puffy labia, lingering there long after the flesh was dry. Her clitoris answered their efforts by throbbing repeatedly.

They led her out of the bathhouse. It was as though they had made her light; she hardly felt her feet touching the ground. Perhaps they carried her, she didn't know. She did know that what they had pressed into her sex was still there, its presence a constant provocation.

She found herself in a short, white marble corridor, off which, on both sides, were large open cubicles. She was taken into the nearest. The cubicle was featureless, apart from a low, wooden slatted frame about twice the width of a double bed, and covered with a thin cream-coloured mattress. In the centre of the mattress was a hand-carved wooden block, its shape exactly like the impression of a bottom pressed into sand, two deep hollows separated by a thick ridge in the centre.

The four pairs of ebony black hands pulled

Melinda down on to the frame, turning her on her back so her fleshy buttocks fitted into the wooden block. This had two effects. It arched her body like a bow, up off the frame, so her belly was at the highest point and her labia were angled upwards. And it also parted and separated her buttocks. The way the hollows were carved in relation to each other stretched them apart, forcing her sex open.

Melinda had no need to wonder what they were going to do to her. It was perfectly obvious. The moment they had her lying flat on the frame it began. Bandu knelt between her open legs, stroked the light fleece of her upturned pubis, then lowered her head so she could kiss her labia, kissing them like a mouth, squirming her lips against them. Then her tongue darted out, probing between them. It instantly found its target. Melinda moaned as she felt the hot wet tongue flicking at her already engorged clit, pushing it from side to side.

It was as if the noise she made was a signal for the other three. They knelt on the mattress and, as Bandu's tongue continued its work, Melinda felt them descend on her body, three mouths and six hands, kissing and sucking and kneading and pinching at every inch of her flesh. Fingers pawed her breasts and pinched her nipples, a mouth sucked her toes while another kissed and nibbled her neck and invaded the contours of her ear with a tongue. Hands smoothed over her belly and her thighs.

She felt a hand travelling under her leg, up to her buttocks, searching for the entrance to her anus. Finding it, tilted up like the rest of her sex and at the edge of the wooden block, a finger penetrated easily, lubricated by the juices that had run out of her. Melinda felt it moving, moving against the object they had inserted in her vagina, separated only by a thin membrane. Another finger – whether from the same hand or a different one Melinda could not tell – plunged into her vagina. She felt it nudge against the hard object, pushing it deeper, pushing it up to the neck of her womb, where previously undisturbed nerves kicked into life.

There were hands and mouths and bodies everywhere; she was drowning in a sea of sensation, gasping for breath. Every nerve in her body was being teased and tortured and provoked. Again she had the feeling of floating, her body so light it could not remain anchored to the mattress.

Relentlessly, Bandu's tongue moved against her clit with a tempo that was tuned to the rhythms of Melinda's body. It was hot, and felt like a flame licking at her. But it was wet, too. Or rather, she was, juices running down between her legs and over the hands that worked so diligently there.

Melinda stretched out, stretching her body, wanting to feel her tendons as taut as her nerves. She opened her legs as wide as they would go, angling her body up towards the four black women, arching herself off the wooden block, wanting them to see her come. She was on the brink, the precipice, of orgasm. What took her over the edge – whether it was the hardness of the object inside her, or the tongue on her clit, or the fingers pressed into the passages of her body front and rear, or the fingernails that pinched her nipple, or the mouth that sucked at her neck – she could not tell. But whatever it was, she was suddenly pitched over and falling down into an endless pit of raw sensation.

They felt her and saw her. They watched as her body shuddered and trembled, but they did not stop.

The tongue continued to press against her clitoris, the hands moved over her body, the mouths licked and sucked her breasts, the fingers worked in both her inner passages.

Did her orgasm end? Again, she could not decide whether the feelings that rolled over her in huge cascading waves were the same orgasm or a new one they had provoked. All she knew was that the waves came again, picking her up like a piece of driftwood on a storm-tossed sea and throwing her about. Every time she thought it would stop, each time she sensed the storm relenting, a sudden provocation – a tongue playing inside her ear, a hand squeezing her breast, a finger turning in her anus – pitched her back into the maelstrom again.

They held her down as she tossed her head from side to side, unable to control the tremors generated by her nerves. Finally, and gradually, the fingers withdrew from inside her, the mouths and hands left her body and the tongue deserted her clitoris.

But it was not the end. Now all the other provocations were gone, the object inside her sex took precedence. Where once it had only been part, now it was the whole. In her imagination it seemed to be growing, throbbing inside her, as hard as stone. She felt her sex squeezing it, contracting around it, as if trying to gauge its size.

Her orgasm had forced her eyes closed but now she managed to open them. She wanted to see the four naked Nubians. They sat around her, all four of them staring at her open and prone body, their black skin making her look alabaster white in contrast.

'Oh,' she gasped. The contractions in her sex were pushing the object out, pushing it down, slippery wet with her juices. It would be expelled, squeezed out, and she knew instinctively that would make her come again. She braced herself, her nerves so overwrought with feeling she wondered if she could bear another climax; not that she had any choice. The muscles of her sex had taken control. The invader was to be expelled. She felt the contractions inching the object down to the lips of her sex. One more now and it would be out. She braced herself, her body rigid. She felt the spasm begin. Her vagina squeezed in and the object shot out, plunging her into a short, sharp orgasm that shook through her body so strongly it was almost like pain. She thought she even screamed, but could not be sure.

It passed quickly. Her muscles, as rigid as steel, were released from its grip and trembled uncontrollably, as a reaction to overuse. She curled herself into a tight ball, the only way, it seemed, to still the tremors that beset her. Strangely, in seconds she felt herself drifting off into a deep sleep. The excitements of the day combined with the extremes of feeling she had just been subjected to, made sleep inevitable.

She had not noticed, in the carefully designed cubicles of the bathhouse – meticulously reproduced on the model of a villa excavated at Herculaneum, as was everything else in the house, down to the very last detail – that recessed at the top of one of the dividing walls was the very un-Roman lens of a video camera, which moved to bring Melinda's body into tight close-up.

Three

The sunlight woke her. It streamed in through a large window which had been glazed in opaque white glass. They must have carried her from the bathhouse into this small room while she was still asleep, as she had no memory of being brought here.

She was lying on a small wooden bed with a rather lumpy straw palliasse. The room was more or less square with a single door. On the floor, next to the door, was an earthenware jug of water and a plate, also made from rough terracotta, on which was some bread and cheese, and some cold meat.

Melinda ate hungrily as she examined the room more closely. In one corner there was a modern chrome shower head with taps underneath it. To the side of this was a small toilet. The floor of the room was wooden.

After she had finished the food and drunk up the water, Melinda used the toilet and showered. The water was cold, but as the room was warm it was not an unpleasant feeling. There was no towel, but in the heat of the room it did not take long for her to dry off naturally. As the sun rose, the temperature in the room increased rapidly.

From the other side of the window Melinda could hear the noise of slaves being taken off to work and the occasional clatter of hooves on paving-stones. She could hear, too, the noise of people diving into the swimming pool she had seen last night, so, she reasoned, her room must be just off the atrium.

Despite all the comings and goings outside, no one came for Melinda. Hour followed hour. She was forgotten.

It was a familiar pattern. There were variations in every Master's household, but the underlying routine was the same. The new slave was always left waiting, hanging on tenterhooks, wondering when the new Master would be ready to see her. Here, her initial reception, the incredible sexual experience the four Nubian women had given her, had been designed specifically to make the neglect more noticeable in comparison. This reminded her, as if she needed reminding, that what the Master had the power to grant he could just as easily deny.

Melinda now had little doubt that whoever had abducted her was part of the OIM. Though she had convinced herself that the explanation for her kidnap was impatience, she was aware that she might be wrong. It was possible the whole thing was some sort of test designed by the OIM, though what sort she could not imagine. Whatever happened, she would be careful to obey. After her experience in Paris she did not want another bad mark against her.

As the light began to fade, food was pushed through the door by a man in a Roman tunic who said nothing. He took the empty jug and plate left over from the morning. The sun seemed to set rapidly and the room was soon dark, apart from the odd shaft of light momentarily flickering from under the door as someone passed by, perhaps with a candle.

There was nothing for Melinda to do but lie on the

bed. Though she was not in the least bit tired, having done nothing all day, she fell asleep almost at once.

Again, after a long and apparently dreamless sleep, she was woken by the sun. She found food had been placed on the floor by the door, and no one came for her.

She heard the slaves going off to work and, at some time in the morning, she thought she could make out, distant but distinct, the whistle of a whip and the anguished cries of a female slave. She heard other voices, too. It was as though the whipping was being viewed by others. She imagined Bandu, whip in hand, muscles rippling and eyes sparkling. The thought made Melinda shudder, not entirely from fear.

With nothing to do, her mind wandered. She tried to think why the OIM would want to trick her into thinking she had been kidnapped. In Paris with her last Master, she had been forced to break the most basic rule of the organisation after that of total obedience. She had spoken out to reveal a treachery within the Countess's household. Perhaps all this was an elaborate ruse to test her obedience after this breach, to make sure she was still suitable to be a slave and still honoured her commitment to obey.

But the more she thought about it, the more unlikely it seemed. If they wanted to test her obedience there were far better ways for them to do it. Besides, being ostensibly kidnapped – pulled, as far as she knew, out of the control of the OIM – would give her every right to disobey, on the grounds that she was no longer controlled by a proper Master. The logic of this, together with the fact that Sophia had not given her the slightest hint that anything but the normal transfer was about to take place, made Melinda convinced that wherever she was now and whoever was behind her abduction had nothing to do with any plot devised by the OIM.

However, it was perfectly clear – from everything she had seen and from the way she had been treated so far – that this place and its owner was part of the OIM. For a start, there were all the other slaves she had seen, and the size of the establishment. Members of the OIM had to have enough wealth to provide a house in a suitable position, with absolute security and privacy, and the villa had obviously been constructed with these requirements in mind. On top of that, the man in charge was only too familiar with OIM patterns – the softening-up process all the Masters adopted to make the slaves grateful for even the tiniest amount of time, and contact, and to make them needy and responsive.

The owner of this villa had either broken away from the OIM, or was still part of it but preferred to take matters into his own hands. Whichever applied, Melinda knew she had no reason to obey his commands. Her allegiance was to the OIM. She could refuse to co-operate with this man's plans; she could demand to be taken back to the halfway house. There were two very good reasons why she was not going to do that, however. First, there was a real and tangible threat of punishment. She was sure this Master had ways to punish her quite as frightening as any she had come across with the others. Second, she would not disobey because of the excitement she had felt from the first moment she had been bundled into the car, excitement that had only been enhanced by her treatment at the villa.

Despite the kidnapping – probably precisely *because* of it – her sexual needs had increased along with her isolation. The feelings the four Nubians had created in her body still lingered like shadows and refused to disappear. She was incredibly aware of the nakedness of her body, of her breasts and nipples – which seemed to be permanently erect – and of her softly furred labia. She needed and craved contact, both human and sexual.

She also wanted to meet the Master. She needed a Master. She had to have someone to control her. The role she had chosen for herself was not accidental: she as a slave because that was exactly what she wanted to be. If her new Master (whoever and whatever he might be) had picked her out, if he had wanted her so much he had broken the rules and had had her abducted, if he was so anxious to have her, then why didn't he show himself? She knew the answer. He would show himself when he felt Melinda was ready; when she was soft and ripe like a peach, ready to obey and give herself to him, desperate for his slightest attention.

Food arrived as the light began to fade. Melinda ate it unenthusiastically; it looked as though she was doomed to another night languishing in her cell. She lay the tray by the door when she had finished and settled down on the bed.

Only minutes after she'd done so, Melinda heard the door being unbolted, and the room flooded with light from a source hidden discreetly in the ceiling. Bandu strode into the room. She was dressed in dark brown leather: a skirt divided into long rectangular tongues of leather and a leather halter-neck top that fitted over her breasts but left her navel bare. Her feet were clad in tight leather Roman boots, open sandal-like straps with a series of loops up around the back of the calf supporting a tapering strip of stiffened leather down the front of the shin. She was carrying a white robe over her arm.

'You put this on,' Bandu said, throwing the robe down on the bed.

Melinda got to her feet, her heart pounding. There could only be one reason for Bandu's presence. She was being taken to the Master.

Trying to control her emotions, Melinda picked up the white robe. It was a simple toga made from a light, silky and completely transparent material. On its single shoulder-strap was pinned a large, circular gold brooch. She pulled the robe over her head and, as its folds dropped around her body, she saw it was ankle-length. Even though her body was quite clearly visible through the robe, it felt strange being dressed after such a long time naked.

'You behave. It is better for you.' Bandu looked at her sternly, looking right into Melinda's eyes as if to reinforce the message. 'Follow . . .'

The black woman marched out of the room with Melinda at her heels. They turned out of the short corridor into a much more spacious hall, and were obviously now in the main villa. Doric columns ran along either side of the walls at regular intervals, and the floor and walls were lined with an unusual orange and black striated marble. They turned right, through a pillared arch and into a room the size of the auditorium of a small theatre. It even looked like a theatre: at the far end was a raised platform like a stage. The whole room was lined in marble, this time a subtle grey and white colouring. Along the walls was a trough filled with water and aquatic plants. Right in the centre, a small fountain – a reproduction of the she-wolf being suckled by Romulus and Remus – showered water into the air. Wrought-iron candle-holders bestrode the water trough, supporting the massive honey-coloured candles that gave off the same peculiar odour Melinda had noticed in the bathhouse. But the room was also lit by more modern means, too; some sort of electric light concealed in the ceiling.

The Nubian led Melinda up to the rostrum, the leather soles of her boots slapping against the marble floor. Symmetrically placed in front of the raised platform was a simple stone bench.

'Sit,' Bandu ordered.

Melinda obeyed.

On the platform itself was a dais made from black marble, reached by means of steps that surrounded it on all sides. On the dais was a high-backed chair carved from white stone with scrolled arms, its position and size suggesting a throne. It was scattered with cushions made from a material that shone like gold. Behind the platform, on either side of the throne, was an arch curtained in a rich, red silk, the pillars supporting the stone span sculpted caryatids of female figures in full flowing robes.

There were stone steps leading up to the rostrum on both corners and Bandu mounted them, disappearing behind the drapery on the left-hand arch.

Melinda's excitement was increasing. She really was going to meet the Master at last. She marvelled at the size of the room and what it must have cost to reproduce such an Roman edifice in marble and stone. It was an impressive setting for her initiation.

From somewhere behind her, footsteps approached, together with a babble of conversation in a mixture of languages, some Italian, French and even English. Not daring to look round, she couldn't tell how many people had walked up to stand behind her, but she guessed there were ten or twelve.

The curtains on one of the arches were pulled aside

by some sort of pulley arrangement, which gathered them up into a rope tieback against the caryatid pillar. An ornate, open sedan chair immediately appeared, its frame decorated in gold leaf, its four corners borne, at shoulder height, by the four Nubian women, their bodies draped with diagonally placed leopard skins.

Sitting in the chair was a tall, weighty man, his thinning grey hair combed forward in the Roman style and curled at the front, his heavy body robed in a white toga trimmed with gold thread. He wore a crown of laurels on his head and a huge gold signet ring on his left hand. In his other hand, he carried a gold baton topped with a cast of a Roman eagle.

In perfect synchronisation, the Nubian women swung the supports of the chair from their shoulders to their waists, and then to the floor, barely jolting its occupant at all. As soon as it was grounded, they dropped to one knee and lowered their heads.

The man got to his feet, gathered up the material of his toga to prevent himself tripping over it, and mounted the steps to the throne. He was wearing white leather sandals.

As he mounted the dais, the crowd behind Melinda fell silent. Having reached the throne, he turned to face them. For the first time Melinda felt his power and authority, which radiated from him like heat from the sun. He raised his baton and spoke. Melinda did not recognise the language but thought, as she could make out the odd word, that it might be Latin.

After a minute, he stopped. The crowd had been hanging on his every word, and applauded the moment he had finished.

His eyes turned to Melinda. It was like being lit up by a powerful searchlight. He looked right through her, and into her innermost secrets. They were icy blue.

'Child,' he said. 'I am Tiberius Julius Caesar Augustus. The Emperor Tiberius, I am called. You must kneel before me.' The man sat on the throne.

Obediently, Melinda slipped off the bench and on to her knees, her heart thumping hard against her ribs. The man was perhaps not conventionally handsome, but there was no doubt about his magnetism or the strength of his personality.

'You are now a slave of the Roman Empire...' His voice was unexpectedly high and reedy considering his bulk; it did not seem to fit the man. '... The greatest civilisation known to man. Wine...' he said, looking around. One of the Nubian women got off her knees and produced a gold, bejewelled chalice, which she filled with red wine from a tear-shaped earthenware bottle balanced on a metal stand that stood on a small table at the back of the rostrum. Bowing deeply, she handed the chalice to the Emperor, then resumed her position at the sedan chair.

The Emperor drank the wine. A little escaped the corner of his mouth and ran down his chin, but he did not bother to wipe it away. 'You are from Britannia?' For a moment Melinda did not know what he meant. 'Answer, child.' The rebuke was so strong it was almost like being slapped in the face.

'Yes, Master.'

'Well, in Rome you will find things very different from your heathen ways. You are savages, with no knowledge of civilisation. You must forget your past and learn new ways. Do you understand?'

'Yes, Master.'

'That is good. You will be put to the test. If you pass, you will become one of my nine body slaves.

You will serve me and, occasionally, my special guests.' He stood up and clapped his hands loudly.

Immediately, the curtains on the other arch were drawn back. Two women came running out on to the platform. They were both naked. One was curvaceous, with big pendulant breasts and a full fleshy arse, her long blonde hair streaming down her back. The other was the complete opposite, her body slender, with no tits to speak of, very small nipples and buttocks that were flat and hard. In fact, as her dark hair was also cut short, but for the fact she did not have a penis sprouting from her dark pubic hair, the second woman could well have been a boy.

The two women lay on their stomachs, stretched across the steps of the throne, their hands reaching for the Emperor's feet, which they then kissed. Then they raised their heads, waiting for instructions.

'Proceed,' he said.

The darker boy-like woman crawled on her belly up on to the dais and around behind the Emperor. She put her head up under the toga and Melinda could see it moving along his legs to his buttocks. The more voluptuous of the pair crawled forward, too, inserting her head under the front of the toga, licking and kissing his thighs until she reached his crotch, where it was clear she then concentrated on his cock.

'Tomorrow,' the Emperor continued, as the two women worked on him, 'you will be put to the test of obedience. It is a test I have devised and is most severe. I demand absolute submission. If you fail, you will serve the Empire of Rome in more menial ways. You will toil in the gardens and be used by the guests and overseers for their amusement as they see fit. You do not wish to fail, do you, child?'

'No, Master.'

'I hope you will not fail. I have gone to a lot of trouble to bring you here. Tiberius does not like failure. My commanders who fail me in battle meet a fate worse than death. That is why they fight so fiercely. Of course, sometimes, even if they succeed ... *pour encourager les autres* ...' He found this remark extremely funny and laughed loudly.

He looked down at Melinda again, his icy blue eyes looking straight into hers. There was an expression on his face she could not properly describe. It was not sexual excitement, it was not lust; it was maniacal. From what she could remember reading about Tiberius, he was mad, throwing both friends and enemies from precipitous cliffs and devising elaborate tortures which his guests were made to watch while they ate dinner.

This man was certainly playing the role well; so well, in fact, that Melinda wondered if his grip on reality was all that secure, whether he could distinguish any longer between the part he was playing and the person he had once been. The glint in his eyes, and the way he seemed to savour every word he pronounced, suggested that he could not. Melinda now had another good reason for not contemplating disobedience or demanding to be returned to the OIM. Her new Master, she was becoming rapidly convinced, was as mad as the Emperor he impersonated.

'My robe,' he commanded.

The boyish woman emerged from the folds of the garment, took the white material and pulled it up over the Emperor's body, bunching it together so she could pull it over his head without disturbing the laurel crown. As the garment rose, it revealed the long-haired blonde woman kneeling in front of her Master, his cock buried in her mouth.

The Emperor's body was tanned. Though it looked as though it had once been hard and strong, it was now running to fat, mostly around his portly gut. Following the Roman fashion, his body was hairless (apart from his pubes), treated with wax and rubbed with body oil to give it a rather feminine sheen.

As soon as the toga had been discarded, the dark-haired woman returned to her position of kneeling behind the Emperor. Melinda watched as she tongued his buttocks, working her mouth lower until she could get her tongue right into the little bud of his anus.

'Now, I think it is time I showed you what happens to disobedient slaves.' He clapped his hands twice. Immediately, the Nubians jumped to their feet and ran through one of the arches. In seconds they had returned, bearing on their shoulders a rectangular frame, two long parallel wooden beams bound by leather thongs to two shorter ones, their corners overlapping. Spread-eagled face down on the frame, with her wrists and ankles tied to each corner, was a naked woman, her big breasts rubbing together as she was moved.

In the floor of the platform there were two square holes, the exact profile of the wooden beams. The Nubians slotted the ends of the long beams of the frame into the holes and hoisted it up until the frame was vertical, the beams fitting tightly into the square receptacles.

For a moment, Melinda had thought the Nubians had made a mistake. They had turned the frame so the X of the woman's body was now upside down, her long black hair sweeping the marble floor, her open and exposed sex at just below head height.

But it was not a mistake.

'Speak your crimes and beg your Emperor's forgiveness.' Tiberius' voice echoed around the marble hall.

Melinda heard a voice and the crack of a whip behind her and dared to sneak a look. The overseers were ushering in the working slaves, obviously so they could witness the punishment.

'Please . . .' the bound woman said, in an English voice.

'Speak your crimes and beg.' The Emperor pushed the two body slaves away and walked down the steps of the throne, his big circumcised cock bobbing out in front of him. He stood within feet of the captive. 'Well, I'm waiting. Do you want to keep the Emperor waiting?'

'I disobeyed an order, Master . . . please don't punish me again.'

'Who am I?' He moved closer, so close his cock nudged against the upturned woman's body.

'Tiberius. The Emperor Tiberius.'

'And . . .'

'You are Tiberius the Great, Tiberius the Noble, the greatest Emperor in the history of Rome.'

'Go on . . .'

'Please don't punish me like this.'

'And?' he insisted angrily. 'What order did you disobey?'

'I . . . I . . .'

'Come on.'

'It was too big, Master. I couldn't take it. I tried, but it was too big.'

'He was my guest.'

'I tried Master.'

'Ten lashes.'

'No!' The woman's scream rang around the hall.

'Do you want more?'

'No. No. Please...'

'Bring the slaves in close so they may see the cost of disobedience in the Roman Empire.'

The overseers hustled the slaves towards the rostrum. The guests came closer, too. Melinda looked into the woman's eyes. As much as she heard terror in her voice, as much as she twisted and turned against her bonds, her hair sweeping the floor, she could see that the woman's eyes were filled with another emotion, with the flame of excitement, just as Melinda's would have been in the same situation.

One of the Nubians had brought a small urn full of water. Another had carried in a wooden block, which was placed behind the woman's head. The first Nubian stood on it, raised the urn between her tethered legs and poured its contents down over the woman's open sex. Water cascaded down all over her body. Another of the black women advanced, carrying a short leather whip. She took the place of the first Nubian on the block and immediately brought the whip slashing down on the inside of the woman's thigh.

'One,' the captive shouted out at the top of her voice, knowing it was a requirement. The whip was aimed again, this time landing on the other thigh, narrowly missing her labia. 'Two,' the woman intoned again.

Her naked breasts were quivering. Melinda suddenly noticed that although they were inverted, hanging down towards her chin, the flesh underneath her breasts was unmarked. She did not have the little purple squares that all the slaves of the OIM were given by their first Masters.

The whip cracked down again. Red weals appeared

on her inner thighs. Every time the whip landed, a new weal appeared. Every time the woman shouted out a number, her voice became more stretched and hoarse.

At five, the Emperor raised his hand to call a halt. The whipping had noticeably increased the size and hardness of his cock. The Nubian moved aside, allowing him to come around and mount the wooden block. He ran his hand over the plane of the woman's sex which was covered with a thick mat of black curly hair. Melinda saw him dip a finger down, penetrating her vagina.

'Oh, Master . . .' she gasped.

He withdrew his finger, wet with her juices and prodded it forward until it was nudging her clitoris. She moaned again, raising her head to try and see her sex, her neck muscles knotted by the effort.

'Please, Master,' she begged.

'What do you want, slave?'

'Punish me, Master . . .'

The Emperor withdrew his hand and stepped down from the block. As soon as the Nubian had replaced him, five more blows from the thin lashes of the whip fell on her inner thighs, working ever closer to her delicate labia but never actually making contact. The woman writhed against her bonds; the whip created a need that she had no way of satisfying.

'Ten,' she cried, her frustration more and more evident.

The Nubian stepped off the block, her job complete.

'Please, Master, please,' the woman begged.

'But your punishment is over. You asked me to punish you and I have given you what you wanted. What can you want now?' the Emperor taunted, climbing up on to the wooden block again, cock in hand. The height of the block was sufficient to allow him to slide his erection forward directly between her labia, until the glans poked out in front of her.

'Yes, Master, yes,' she moaned.

'You.' The Emperor addressed the boyish body slave, beckoning her to stand in front of the captive's body. 'Suck it,' he said.

The body slave obeyed at once, bending slightly to wrap her lips around the Emperor's cock, at least as much of it as protruded from the inverted sex of the brunette.

The Emperor turned his attention to Melinda. Again she felt as if she was suddenly illuminated by a powerful spotlight.

'Stand up,' he ordered.

Melinda jumped to her feet.

'So you see, my child,' he was staring into her eyes, 'I am the Emperor of all I survey. I have the ultimate power; to give pleasure and to take it away.' As if to demonstrate what he meant, he pulled his cock away from the body slave's mouth and the brunette's sex, then returned it again. 'My word is law.' His eyes looked at the assembled crowd whose eyes were all watching the bizarre spectacle with rapt interest. The body slave sucked hard on his glans. He felt the wetness of the captive's labia along the underside of his phallus. The idea – of power, of having dominion over his Empire, of the slaves watching and fearing that he would turn his attention on them and that they would be bound and whipped or worse – turned him on. 'My power . . . The Emperor's power . . .'

At that moment, he pushed the body slave's mouth away. As he plopped out of her mouth, a string of white spunk jetted from the eye of his cock. The woman had felt his prick spasming against her sex. She raised her head again just in time to catch the spunk in her face and even captured some in her mouth. She was so close, so frustrated; this was enough. As she watched her Master's cock jerking above, her sex began to convulse. The completion she had been denied for so long was at last triggered by the thought that her Master was allowing her such intimacy.

Four

Melinda was naked again. Two of the Nubians led her out of the house and into the atrium. The moon was almost full: only the slightest edge was missing from the complete circle. The night air was balmy and scented with flowers; the trickle of water coming from the swimming pool was the only noise.

They took her over to a flat stone set at about forty-five degrees to the ground, pointing towards the balcony of what, from its size and position, was obviously the Emperor's bedroom. One of the Nubians carried a heavy leather belt which she quickly wrapped around Melinda's waist and buckled it tight. Hanging down from the front of the belt was a heavy chain, each link at least the width of a finger. She adjusted the belt until the chain hung directly between Melinda's legs.

Pushing her back against the stone, the Nubians manacled her wrists and ankles to metal rings set in each corner of the rectangular surface.

'Sleep well,' one of the Nubians said, patting the hard stone and smiling to her companion. As an afterthought, she leant forward and pushed the metal chain against Melinda's sex, making contact with her clitoris. Then they walked away.

Melinda looked up at the moon poised above the

roof of the villa. Her whole body was still trembling from the thrills she had felt in the hall. The Master had performed for her; he had indulged himself to teach *her* a lesson. Whether he was sane or not, whether he really believed he was Tiberius, didn't matter at the moment. What mattered was the attention he had paid her. She knew now she had not been kidnapped by chance. The Master had told her he had wanted her specifically. Her theory was right. He must have seen her on the OIM video link from Paris and planned the abduction accordingly.

In a world where normal emotions were suspended, where the slightest crumb of comfort was blown out of all proportion, Melinda's emotions were not subject to the normal rules. She lived in a world where slaves competed for the Master's time, in a world where Masters were too busy – or pretended to be too busy – to care for their slaves and where, therefore, such single-minded determination to own one particular slave among so many set Melinda's pulse racing. She knew, logically, that she should not treat the Emperor as she would one of the other Masters, that he was beyond the pale and had offended the code of behaviour by which the others lived. Unfortunately, her emotions were not governed by logic. She could not control herself; at least, not for the moment. Later, perhaps, she would be able to think more clearly, to plan properly what she must do, to work out where her loyalties lay. But that was not possible now, as every nerve in her body seemed to be responding to a more fundamental impulse; her need to be special and her desire to be mastered.

She could see lights in what was obviously *his* bedroom, though most of the rest of the villa was dark. She saw a shadow crossing the windows, draped, as they were, in a thin white muslin. She imagined it was the Master.

The links of the chain pressed into her sex, cold and heavy. She was stimulated enough by the images in her mind, but the chain and her bondage made it worse. Her imagination was freed by her excitement: her mind raced over the fate that awaited her, wild flights of fancy as to what test the Master had conjured up.

Melinda's body had already passed beyond the threshold of control. Bound tightly to the angled stone, she was no longer tethered by mental constraints that told her she could only come if she was commanded to do so. She wanted to come, no matter what the price or punishment. She could even tell herself that what happened at the villa was not covered by her vows of obedience, but that was a poor excuse.

The Emperor was a cunning Master. He had calculated exactly the effect he would have on her body and on her mind. After two days of isolation and neglect, the impact of the spectacle she had seen was extreme. Had she been returned to her cell and left unfettered she would have been unable to stop herself from satisfying the needs he had created. Bound to the cold stone, she had no such freedom, although it did not decrease the desire. Indeed, the bondage and the deliberately placed chain resting against her sex increased her longing.

The chain was insidious. It insinuated itself between her thighs, as she, almost unconsciously, wriggled her body against it. Slowly the weight of the metal, and her own movement, parted her labia and exposed the swollen nut of her clitoris, making matters worse.

If only she could have held it there. If she could

have closed her thighs on the links, squeezed her buttocks together to put pressure on her labia and held the metal against her clitoris, it would have been enough. In a matter of seconds she would have been at the brink of orgasm and then over it. But she could not. Her legs were manacled too far apart and too tightly to allow the necessary movement. All she could do was move the links of the chain from side to side by squirming her bottom against the stone. It was enough to stimulate her further, but not enough to relieve her frustration. In fact her aggravation increased. At one moment the metal seemed perfectly placed, rubbing exactly the right spot, but, just as she felt her body respond, she would move involuntarily and it would slip away, leaving her beside herself with disappointment.

It was deliberate. The man who believed he was the Emperor Tiberius had planned it perfectly, executing the philosophy of the OIM. A slave was never allowed to choose her own fate; her ability to achieve completion, like everything else, was solely dependent on her Master. He had decreed that she should not be allowed to come tonight and, whatever she cared to do, she could not and would not.

After what seemed like hours of fruitless effort to persuade or trick or cajole her body into orgasm, Melinda must have finally fallen asleep, though only into a light, fitful slumber. She was not quite sure whether she was dreaming when she saw the dawn break over the buildings that surrounded the courtyard. The Emperor stepped, naked, on to his balcony and stared down at her helpless body. She could see his cock, erect in his hand as he caressed it lightly. Real or not, the next time she opened her eyes, he was gone.

The activity in the pool woke her up again. She watched two of what she presumed to be guests – a man and a woman – come out of the villa and dive into the water, which, in the slight chill of the early morning, produced a light mist like steam. Both were naked and overweight. They swam lazily up and down the length of the pool, then pulled themselves out and dried themselves on big green towels.

'Let's look,' Melinda heard the woman say.

'I'm hungry,' the man protested. Their voices were both English.

But the woman had already walked over to the slanted stone on which Melinda was spread, and was wrapping the towel around her body. 'She's beautiful,' she said, leaning forward to move the chain out from between Melinda's legs so she could see her labia.

'Mmm,' the man mumbled as he got closer.

'Can I touch?'

'Guess so.'

The woman leant forward and slipped her hand around one of Melinda's breasts. The man was still drying his hair. Melinda saw his cock stir as the woman's hand slipped down to the light fleece of Melinda's belly. One of her fingers poked her labia.

'She's wet,' the woman commented.

'Is she?' the man's interest was increasing with his erection.

'Very.' Melinda felt the finger probe lower and push into her sex.

'Perhaps we'll get a chance at her if she fails the test.'

'I'm ... I'd like that. We could have her between us.'

'Meantime...' The man came up behind the

woman and pulled the towel away from her body. He stuck his erection between her substantial buttocks and bucked his hips slightly. Melinda could see the woman's face change, softening with pleasure as he pushed his cock inside her.

'Oh, so good. Are you imagining it's her?'

'I'm imagining it's both of you.'

'What would you do?' The woman's finger was still inside Melinda's sex. If she held it there much longer Melinda would be able to come . . .

'I'd watch while she kissed every inch of your body.'

'Oh, it sounds lovely.'

'Let's do it.'

'Now?'

'I'll get one of the other slaves.'

'Go on then.'

The woman pulled her finger out from Melinda's sex and turned, kissing her partner on the mouth and writhing her fat body against him. Hand in hand they walked towards the slaves' quarters.

The incident only served to renew Melinda's frustration. She could feel the impression of the woman's finger inside her body, though it had not gone very deep. It had set her body on edge again just as it had relaxed slightly, making her squirm against the manacles and the heavy chain which had fallen back between her legs.

Gradually the courtyard came to life. Horses were brought out of the stables and saddled up, overseers appeared, leading naked female slaves to work, and more guests came to swim or take coffee by the pool. Some of the guests would walk over to examine Melinda more closely, but she was not touched again.

It was not until the sun was high in the sky and all

the slaves had been taken off to work that two Nubians came out of the house. Dressed in the leather outfit that Bandu had worn, with the sandal boots, they unfastened the manacles that held Melinda so securely. She was led into the bathhouse, where she was allowed to bathe herself in the big tank and use the toilet.

As soon as she was dry, she was taken into the cubicles where a table and chair had been set up and food provided. One of the Nubians stood in the doorway as Melinda ate.

The food was cleared away but no one appeared in any hurry to move Melinda. The other cubicles appeared to be deserted. Apart from the regular breathing of her black observer there was not a sound. Every so often another Nubian would come to relieve her companion. They were working in shifts to watch Melinda.

Time passed slowly. With nothing to do, Melinda's mind wandered. She began to think about Sophia and the halfway house and about the punishment of the female slave on the rostrum last night. She thought about the way the woman had touched her this morning. Her body, stilled temporarily by her bath, began to churn again. She shifted in the wooden seat of the chair.

'Stop,' the Nubian barked, leaping forward and slapping her hand down on the top of the table so suddenly that it made Melinda jump. 'Not allowed.'

Melinda watched the black woman resume her position at the doorway of the cubicle, leaning against the wall. The leather tongues of the skirt parted to reveal her broad thighs, the muscles forming strong, hard contours under the flesh. Above the waist of the skirt her navel was equally hard, and flat.

The tight leather halter was moulded to her small pert breasts. Melinda thought she could see the outline of her nipples under the brown leather. She wondered what it would be like to press herself against such an athletic body, how it would feel. She imagined that hard thigh pushing up between her legs, the iron muscle against her soft sex, those powerful arms embracing her, crushing her, her spongy breasts compressed between their bodies. She imagined being forced down to lick and suck at her sex, while she was lifted bodily and lowered on to the Nubian's face...

'Stop!' The Nubian slapped the table again, bringing Melinda smartly back to reality.

It did not stop her imagination, but she was careful not to translate the daydreams she was having into bodily movements, however much she craved the comfort of being able to subtly rub her thighs together.

It was all part of the test, of course. *He* knew that after so long without fulfilment she would be able to think of nothing but her body and her sex. Whatever lay ahead for her, the test had already began.

It was dark when, after the Nubians had changed shifts several times, Bandu finally came for her. 'It is time,' she said. 'Stand.'

Melinda obeyed. She saw Bandu looking critically at her naked body. She extended her hand and flicked at both of Melinda's nipples, bringing them to full erection and sending a shudder through Melinda's body that made her moan. Equally casually she extended a finger down between Melinda's legs and pressed it into her clitoris.

'No,' Melinda cried, only just stopping herself from trying to wrench Bandu's hand away.

'Good.' Bandu smiled, revealing a line of very white teeth. 'You are ready. Follow.'

She led the way through into the main house, down the marbled hall and past the theatre-like room she had been taken to yesterday. Further on, they came to a broad flight of stone steps which descended into a cellar.

At the bottom of the steps Melinda found herself in a large room divided at regular intervals by pillars supporting the floor above. Unlike everywhere else she had been in the main house, the floor was covered in stone flags and strewn with rugs, all of which, she thought, were of Roman design. The room was lit by the massive candles she had seen upstairs, and, for once, were not supplemented by hidden electric light.

In the flickering glow of the candle flames she could see the Emperor at the far end of the room. One of the other Nubians waited by the stairs and together they led Melinda over to him, but he did not speak or acknowledge her in any way. A tray of food was set out on a small table in front of a sort of *chaise longue* – one end of the long, softly upholstered bench was scrolled up to form a low headrest – where the Master reclined in what looked like a very loose, dark red robe. Two body slaves, both wearing short, white togas, were attending him, one handing him a chalice of wine while the other peeled him a juicy black grape then popped it into his mouth. Melinda recognised the body slave with the grape as the boyish-figured woman from last night.

The Nubians positioned Melinda between two pillars about eight feet away from the *chaise longue*. Attached to each pillar was a metal ring at shoulder height, tied into which was a long white rope. Each of the black women took one of the ropes and tied them around Melinda's wrists until she was stretched tightly between the pillars, her arms at right angles to her body. This done, Bandu produced a long wooden bar about three inches thick, with crescent-shaped notches carved out of each end and around which a thick leather strap was secured. Dropping to her knees, Bandu fitted the first notch around Melinda's left ankle and buckled the leather strap tight, holding the wood in place. She then pulled Melinda's legs apart so the right ankle could be fitted into the other side and strapped tight, making it impossible for Melinda to close her legs. The bondage immediately stoked the fires of Melinda's already overheated body; she felt a surge of pleasure.

The body slaves hadn't taken the slightest notice of what was going on and neither had the Emperor. He lay languidly on the *chaise*, allowing one of the slaves to tip the chalice of wine against his lips while the other sliced him a peach.

Bandu and the other Nubian waited to see if the Emperor was going to dismiss them. To their disappointment, he waved them away with his hand.

'Enough,' the Emperor said, after he had consumed most of the peach, its juices running down his chin. The tallest of the two body slaves, a redhead, got to her feet immediately, picked up the tray of food and carried it away, while the boyish slave began to open the dark red robe, exposing the Emperor's belly and his flaccid cock. She pulled the robe from his shoulders as he leant forward to allow her to strip it away altogether.

Leaning back again, he rested his head on the scrolled arm and stared at the ceiling. 'It's time for the test,' he said, his high voice echoing around the cellar. He did not look at Melinda as he spoke.

The redhead returned. She had a curvaceous figure, big breasts billowing out from under the toga and broad, fleshy thighs. She was carrying a small metal bowl, perforated with holes around its upper edge, in which sat a shallow candle. She had another earthenware bowl in her other hand. Setting both bowls down on the table, she took a taper, lit it from the nearest candle, then applied the flame to the candle in the bowl. As soon as it was alight, she placed the earthenware bowl on top of it. The bowl contained a transparent liquid.

'Plania,' the Emperor announced.

'Yes, Master,' the boyish body slave replied.

'You may be the first.'

'Oh, thank you, Master,' she said, with real gratitude.

She knelt on the floor in front of the couch and gently fed the Emperor's still unaroused cock into her mouth. She was remarkably masculine. Kneeling as she was, facing away from Melinda, her slender back and small buttocks could so easily have belonged to a boy. The orgies of ancient Rome had frequently been bisexual; perhaps this was the Emperor's way of recreating them without wanting to introduce real boys.

'Now, Sulpicia,' the Emperor said quietly. The redhead dipped her hands into the earthenware bowl and rubbed her fingers together, coating them with a thick glutinous oil. She transferred her hands to the Emperor's chest, rubbing the oil over his nipples and ribs. Satisfied that he was well-coated in that area, she went to the bowl again for another libation of the warm oil, which this time she smeared on his rotund belly. Soon the front of his body glistened with oil in the flickering light.

'Plania.' It must have been a well-practised routine, for he needed to give no other instructions. Plania pulled her mouth from his cock, which was still not fully erect. She got to her feet and dipped her hands in the warm oil, coating them thickly before returning to wrap them both around his phallus. She massaged the oil into his glans and shaft while Sulpicia began to work on his thighs, kneeling on the other side of the *chaise longue*. Her hands insinuated upwards until she was rubbing the oil against his balls.

Melinda was so fascinated watching this ritual that she had almost forgotten her own feelings; that is, until the sight of the Master's cock being so thoroughly manipulated stirred them anew. But the surging need she had felt seemed to be much less under control, much more urgent, any momentary pause only serving to fuel her desire. Her tightly bound body, stretched like a piano string, created a resonance, too, and amplified every feeling.

The body slaves continued their routine. As they caressed and massaged the Emperor's body, they lifted him slowly into a sitting position on the flat end of the *chaise*. As soon as this was done, Sulpicia went to stand with the back of her knees resting against the scroll of padding. Then, like the beginning of a limbo dance, she leant backwards until her body was draped over the *chaise*, her head and most of her torso on the flat seat, her legs curled up and over the arms, her pubis at the highest point, although, because of her height, her feet still just touched the ground.

The Emperor knelt on the seat, positioning his knees on either side of Sulpicia's head and facing her body. She began to lick the length of his cock, big, long, wet licks which took in his balls, too.

Plania dipped her hands into the oil again and applied a generous lather to his shoulders and back, and down over his buttocks.

Melinda watched as his hairless body was coated with oil. She saw his hands pull the toga on Sulpicia's awkwardly bent body down over her inverted hips to reveal a wiry red forest of pubic hair. But he made no attempt to touch her, or her big breasts which quivered from side to side under the white material in time to the movement of her head.

She could see his cock was throbbing, its veins reddened. A little rivulet of fluid was running down from his urethra, which had not yet been wiped away by Sulpicia's tongue.

'Like a vixen,' he said. 'Red like a vixen.'

He slowly lowered his head to Sulpicia's pubis. His tongue darted out and explored the red hair. Melinda heard her moan; her body jumped as he found her clitoris.

Plania, meantime, worked her oiled hands down over his buttocks and then between them. With one finger, she sought and found his anus and tested the muscles of his sphincter, which relaxed instantly and she penetrated beyond. It was the Emperor's turn to moan.

As Melinda watched, her body trembled with need. She had never seen a Master touch a slave so intimately. She yearned for it to be her in Sulpicia's place. She seemed able to feel her nipples and sex in detail, feel every line and wrinkle of them, the ring of corrugated flesh that made her nipples hard, her puffy labia, parted slightly, the entrance to her sex open and wet, her juices trickling down on to her thigh. But she could feel Sulpicia's clitoris most of all. It was as though it were alive, squirming to escape the flesh under which it was hidden, trying to be free. Every nerve in her body was as stretched as the tendons of her arms tied tightly apart.

'Enough!' The single word reverberated around the cellar.

Plania extracted her finger from his body and got to her feet as the Emperor, in turn, stood up. Melinda felt a flood of excitement. The interruption could only mean one thing. He was saving himself for *her*!

Tiberius walked over to her bound body and looked directly at her for the first time. He came so close to her that his erection almost touched her belly. Taking her cheeks in one hand, he squeezed them together to make her mouth into the shape of an O. She could smell the sweet scent of the body oil that covered him.

'So, did you enjoy the view?' He released her cheeks.

It was a question. She had to remind herself to answer, so overwhelmed was she with emotions. 'Yes, Master.'

'It is a great privilege to be a body slave, to serve the Emperor of all Romans. You understand?'

It was a great honour to serve a Master, whoever he might be. 'Yes, Master,' Melinda replied, emphatically.

'So pretty,' he said, his cold blue eyes looking down at her body. 'Now, it is time.'

He turned and walked into the shadows thrown by the tall candle-holders. There was a small table against one of the pillars. On it there was a jug of wine and a gold chalice. The Emperor filled the chalice with wine and went back to lie on the *chaise*, putting his feet up, resting his head once again on the scrolled arm and staring at the ceiling. Melinda had the strange feeling that he wanted to stop what was going to happen, but could not bring himself to do it.

Sulpicia was passing a thin but strong gold chain

around Melinda's waist, similar to the one that [held] the jewel on her ankle. Hanging down from the b[ack] of the chain was what looked like a fork which had its middle prong removed. At the tip of each of the remaining prongs was a hole from which hung two similar gold chains. The metal of the prongs had been beaten flat so they were at least half an inch wide, and the whole fork was curved almost into a semicircle.

Plania got to her knees in front of Melinda's naked body and pulled the fork-shaped metal up into her crotch, guiding it over her labia. Then she clipped the two chains from each of the prongs into a wider link, designed for the purpose, on the gold chain around Melinda's waist.

Melinda experienced the most extraordinary sensation. As the chains at the front were tightened, the curved prongs pressed against her labia, pushing them down hard into her pubic bone and forcing her clitoris out into the open, a little tongue of pink flesh surrounded by metal. It started to pulse immediately.

Plania got to her feet and went back to the Emperor. She dipped her hands in the warm oil and began to massage herself with it, smoothing it over her almost featureless breasts and her flat belly. She caressed her inner thighs and buttocks, and used the oil to plaster down her pubic hair. She anointed her rather thin labia, too, before coming to sit on the *chaise* and grasping the Emperor's cock in her oily hand. It had shrunk a little but her nimble fingers soon restored it to its full stature.

Sulpicia had disappeared behind Melinda's back. She returned carrying a long wooden pole, its upper end carved into an unequal V-shape, like a finger and thumb. It was her turn to kneel at Melinda's feet. She screwed this pole into a plate secured to the floor in front of the wooden bar that held Melinda's legs apart and right in the middle of it. By means of a small strap, she then tied the leg spreader to the vertical pole, preventing Melinda from pulling back and away from it. The pole apparently had some sort of telescopic extension which allowed its height to be adjusted precisely. Sulpicia pulled it up until the 'finger' of the carved top pointed between Melinda's legs and the 'thumb' was just in front of her immodestly exposed clit.

Standing up, Sulpicia dipped her hands in the bowl of warm oil and transferred them to the wooden phallus, and then to Melinda's sex. Melinda could not suppress a moan as the oiled finger touched her clit, if only briefly. It seemed to jerk, its usual sensitivity increased tenfold. Involuntarily her hips bucked too and her little nut of nerves was forced against the hard 'thumb' of the wooden phallus as its 'finger' penetrated between her labia. A second surge of indescribable pleasure shot through her. She pulled herself back as though she had been stung.

The Emperor had turned his head round lazily on the scrolled arm to watch. 'Good.' He smiled. 'You are very near the edge, aren't you?'

'Yes, Master,' she said, truthfully.

'And now, as you see, it is so easy to topple yourself over it. All you have to do is press forward and you will get what you so desperately need.' He started to laugh. 'Tell me how your clitoris feels?'

Melinda couldn't think of a way to describe it. 'Exposed, Master.'

'Exposed?'

'Yes, Master.'

'You must not come, my child. That is the test. I have provided you with the means, but your test of obedience demands that you do not use it. Do you understand?'

'Oh, Master.' Melinda suddenly understood. Everything had been designed to make it impossibly easy for her to bring herself off; her body constrained in every direction except that which afforded the greatest temptation. She didn't know how she was going to resist. Plania's fingers were wrapped around the Emperor's cock and were moving up and down on it. Subconsciously, Melinda's body had adopted the same rhythm. It accidentally nudged against the phallus again and produced a shock wave of pleasure which raced into her nerves.

'Do you understand?' the Emperor repeated.

'Yes, Master.'

'That is good. Sulpicia...' He gestured towards the shadows and laid his head back on the scrolled arm.

Sulpicia disappeared behind Melinda's back. When she came back, she was carrying a small glazed ceramic bottle which contained a thick amber liquid and a brush that looked as though it might have been used to paint water-colours. Dipping the brush into the liquid, Sulpicia painted Melinda's nipples with the thick viscous fluid. Her task completed, she put the equipment down and returned to the Emperor. Sitting on the opposite side of the *chaise* from Plania, she began to caress the Emperor's chest.

Melinda wondered what the liquid was for. She soon found out. It was like a varnish and it began to dry immediately, contracting and pulling the puckered flesh of her nipples with it. In seconds, the liquid was as hard as beads of glass, imprisoning her nipples inside. The effect was exactly as if clips had been closed over the tender flesh. Her nipples reacted in the same way, too, flooding her body with sensation – a jolt of pain followed instantly by a tide of pleasure.

'No...' she cried, before she could stop herself. Her whole body felt as though it was melting.

'Yes,' the Emperor said softly.

With iron determination, Melinda clenched every muscle she could, trying desperately not to let her body rock forward on to the waiting phallus. It would only take a few seconds for her clitoris – trapped as it was, as exposed as it ever had been – to bring her to orgasm if it were brushed against the 'thumb' of the pole. The days of frustration, the agony of last night, all the images the Emperor had deliberately fed into her mind – everything combined to enhance her need.

But she was still in control. How she would have loved to let herself go, to push forward and allow her body to take its simple pleasure, to feel her orgasm explode at long last! But she was not going to. She was a slave. She belonged to the OIM and had taken a vow to obey. The fact that she knew Tiberius – or whatever this man was called – had offended against the organisation made her determination stronger, not weaker. Giving in would be the easy way out. She wanted to show herself that even without all the paraphernalia of the organisation she was still a perfect slave, born to submission. In the past, she could be threatened, told that if she did not care to obey she would be banished for ever from the Masters, no longer part of the whole. But this Master held no such threat. He was on his own, a rogue and traitor. The only reason for Melinda to obey here was her own pride; her will to prove her need to obey was greater than her need for anything else.

Of course, there was another motive. She did not

want to be a slave consigned to the gardens and used to give pleasure to the guests. She wanted to be a body slave, and to serve the Emperor. If fate had brought her into this strange world, she was going to use her own determination to secure her rightful place within it.

She pulled against the ropes that held her arms and felt the bite of pain on her wrists and shoulders. She would not take her pleasure.

Plania and Sulpicia knelt on the floor on either side of the Emperor's *chaise longue*. Plania – her short hair and symmetrical features as suggestive of a boy as was her figure – slipped the Emperor's cock into her mouth for the second time that evening. Sulpicia, from the other side, leant forward to suck at his balls. The Emperor opened his legs to allow Sulpicia's hand between his thighs. She found the well-oiled crater of his anus and pressed her finger against the little ring of muscle. It resisted at first, then relaxed, and she plunged her finger into the tight rear passage that Plania's had penetrated not moments before.

They knew what he wanted. Sulpicia moved her head up to his chest and gathered one of his nipples between her teeth, biting it hard before leaning over to pinch the other one, her large breasts squashed against him.

Melinda could see he was coming. She had hoped he was going to save it for her but now realised it was probably going to be used as yet another provocation, an extra part of his test. Almost imperceptibly at first, he began to buck his hips off the *chaise*, pushing his cock in and out of Plania's mouth. He did not attempt to touch her; his hands remained folded behind his head on the scrolled arm.

Suddenly he turned his head to face Melinda. Once

again she felt the power in his eyes. She could see everything there, his lust to be in control, his madness, his authority and pleasure. The latter was so affecting her body that she eased forward on to the phallus but she managed to snatch herself back despite the almost unbelievable wave of pleasure it gave her. He watched her intently, as she battled for obedience. She knew that he was not objective, that he cared and wanted her to pass the test and become his personal slave.

Sulpicia snaked her head back on to his lap. It was time. Plania released his cock from her mouth and instead ran her lips along one side of his pulsing shaft. Sulpicia took the other side so that it looked as if they were trying to kiss each other but his cock was in the way. In unison, their mouths slid up and down his erection, while Sulpicia's finger continued to probe his anus, searching for the little gland she knew would trigger his orgasm.

'Jupiter, great god of light...' the Emperor screamed as Sulpicia's finger nudged the centre of his sexual being and, as he stared straight at Melinda's bound and helpless body, strings of white spunk sprung out of the eye of his cock, over his belly and the faces of the two body slaves.

Seeing this, the temptation to come was almost irresistible. But somehow Melinda held her body back, straining at the ropes that held her. The varnish around her nipples was making them itch; her clitoris felt so swollen and alive it was as though it were a thing apart. How she yearned to feel the release, the so visible relief that the Emperor had experienced.

Slowly, the Master got to his feet, his body glistening with oil in the candlelight.

He stood immediately in front of Melinda. A

dribble of spunk ran down the curve of his belly and he gathered it up with the tip of his finger. He extended his finger to her mouth and she sucked it in eagerly. 'I give you permission,' he said.

The words released Melinda from self-restraint. As she sucked on her Master's finger and tasted his seed, she pushed herself forward on to the phallus, as far forward as she could go. The 'finger' penetrated her labia, the 'thumb' pressed against her exposed clit. She rode it, moving her body back and forth, her clitoris charged with feeling as she gazed straight into the Emperor's eyes. He was smiling, his expression all-knowing, all-powerful. He was the Master of all he surveyed, the Master, indeed, of her orgasm.

'Master...' she whispered, at the exact moment every nerve in her body was hit by a shock of feeling – held back for so long – that rocked her body against her bonds, closed her eyes and pitched her into a crimson pit of pleasure so deep she thought it had no end.

Five

The room was long and narrow. Unlike the rest of the servants' and slaves' quarters it was part of the main house. It had only a single door. This was the Emperor's seraglio, but it was not lush and comfortable. Nine straw palliasses were laid out on the stone floor – five on one side, and four on the other – with a passage between them like a dormitory. There were small square windows, but they were set too high in the wall to see out of.

The Nubian made Melinda wait by the door, while she lit a single candle on one of the massive candleholders. It provided little light and Melinda could only see the shadowy shapes of the women who lay on the mattresses.

She was led over to the unoccupied palliasse.

'Stand,' the Nubian ordered, bringing her to a halt.

Melinda saw her walk over to a small cupboard and extract a round black object and a glass bottle.

Back at Melinda's side, the Nubian gave Melinda the bottle to hold. It had a small brush built into the cork stopper. With both hands free, she unlaced the back of what looked like a leather hood, except that it clearly had no openings for the eyes or mouth. With the hood open, she pulled it over Melinda's head and plunged her into total darkness. But the hood did not go on smoothly; there was something sewn into the front that had to be tugged down over her face. It was only when it cleared her nose that Melinda realised that a large rubber ball was secured inside the leather. As soon as it was in position, the Nubian pushed it against her lips, making it clear that Melinda was expected to take it into her mouth as a gag. The ball was so big it filled her mouth completely.

Melinda felt the hood being laced tightly at the back. The soft leather pulled against the contours of her face, making it impossible for her to expel the gag even slightly. The only opening in the hood was a small double hole at the bottom of a projection that had been designed to fit over the nose.

The Nubian took the bottle from Melinda's hand. The hood made it difficult to hear, too; all sounds were muffled, but Melinda thought she heard a plop as the bottle was uncorked. She started as she felt the bristles of a small brush touch her breast and a liquid dribble over her nipple. The Nubian painted over the hard amber varnish that had hardened over her nipples.

Suddenly Melinda felt a burning heat. Her nipples reacted as the varnish softened. She would have winced had the gag not prevented her. The Nubian's fingers seized each little glass-like bead and pulled it sharply away. Melinda felt a surge of pain followed by a soft glow of pleasure, her nipples warmed by whatever solvent had been used to free the varnish. Strangely, they softened, retracting into the flesh of her breast until they hardly protruded at all.

The Nubian's hands on her shoulders indicated that she wanted Melinda to kneel. There was a manacle and short chain attached to a ring which was set into the stone floor. Melinda felt the cold iron close around her wrist. Without another word, the Nubian left. Melinda heard her footsteps and a puff of breath as she extinguished the candle. The door was closed, then bolted from the outside.

Groping around, Melinda found the edges of the palliasse and lay down. Fortunately – since there was no form of bedding – the room was warm.

She was tired but found it difficult to sleep. Her feelings were in turmoil. If she had not been kidnapped, if she did not believe that she was in some way offending the OIM, she would have found everything that had happened profoundly exciting. It *was* exciting. But the more she thought about it the more she knew it was wrong. It was not within the remit of the OIM and therefore not what she should be doing. Her first loyalty, she knew, was to the organisation and always would be.

At that moment, she reasoned, she had little choice but to go along with the Emperor, to treat him in every way as if he *were* a proper Master. She had seen a madness in his eyes and had no intention of arousing his wrath. There was no telling where that would end. But it was clearly her duty, ultimately, to try to find a means of escape, to find her way back to the organisation and tell them what had happened.

She thought of her original Master, the man who had introduced her to the OIM, and who had first brought her face to face with her submissive needs. It was he who would be most worried; the Master who introduced a slave was always regarded as responsible for them wherever they were sent by the system. By now, presumably, he would have been informed that Melinda had not reached the destination she had been assigned. She only hoped her passivity as the kidnapping was taking place – she had no alternative to passivity, after all: bound, gagged and blindfolded as she'd been – was not taken to mean she had any complicity in the events. Surely they could not possibly think that? The idea made her go cold.

As she lay in the darkness, she thought she heard a jingle of a chain. She listened intently. There was a light footfall of naked feet on the wooden boards; then she felt the warmth of a body kneeling beside her.

'Are you awake?' a female voice asked, a hand touching her arm tenderly.

Melinda nodded.

'Be very quiet. I'm going to take your hood off. Roll over.' The voice had the lilt of an Irish accent.

Melinda rolled on to her back and felt fingers unlacing the leather hood. With great relief, she felt it being pulled away. The gag popped out of her mouth.

Moonlight filtered through the square windows, casting an eerie grey shade on the room. Melinda's eyes were already used to the dark and adjusted quickly. Kneeling in front of her was a small, slender girl with short, layered ginger hair. Her face was creased in a big smile. Her naked body was finely proportioned with a narrow waist, and full spherical breasts that looked like melons.

'Mollie,' she whispered. 'I always like to welcome newcomers.'

Melinda hesitated. The rule of only speaking in response to a question was deeply engrained in her. Though she knew she was no longer under the control of the OIM, and she knew she could speak without fear of the consequences from *them* at least, she still found it difficult to break her rigid training.

'Melinda,' she said. She spoke her own name so

rarely it sounded odd. It implied things about herself – will, ego, individuality – that she had long since given up. 'How did you get free?'

'My parents worked in a circus. I learnt a lot of tricks ... escapology among them. Have you just been given the test?'

'Yes. And you?'

'All the body slaves are given it. There was a vacancy.'

'Vacancy?'

'One of the girls refused to obey one of the Emperor's special guests. He was too big for her.'

Melinda remembered the long-haired brunette who had been punished in the main hall. 'Yes, I think I saw her.'

'Well, she was thrown out, so you are in. You were kidnapped, right?'

'Yes, how did you know?'

'From the halfway house?'

'Yes. Four men in a car.'

'It's happened to two or three of the girls. Me included.' She lifted her fleshy breast, pressing it up towards her chin and exposing a neat purple square with the letter M neatly outlined at its centre.

Melinda heaved a sigh of profound relief, so affecting she wanted to cry. Mollie was part of the OIM. She was not alone. However remotely, she had contact with the organisation again.

'But not all the girls ...?' She remembered that the woman who had been punished had not been marked.

'No. Not all. It's a long story.'

'The Master ... I mean, the Emperor ... he was in the OIM though?'

'Oh yes. He *was*. They threw him out. He refused

to send two of the girls back after the three months.' All the slaves in the OIM were given to a Master for three months. After that they had to be sent on, auctioned off to a new establishment. 'Now he recruits for himself locally. All the girls with Roman names are local – well, Italian. He's got very grandiose schemes. He wants to set up his own organisation, and all the houses have to be Roman. That's going to be a condition of membership apparently. He wants his own empire. I'm sure the man is barking mad.'

'Will he do it?'

'Hasn't had one taker yet. None of the girls here have ever been moved.'

'How long have you been here?'

'Six months.'

The answer depressed Melinda. 'But how did he manage to kidnap us?'

'He's still got the video link on the satellite. Every so often he sees a girl he likes at one of the auctions and sends his hired goons to get her.'

'Haven't the OIM worked it out yet?'

'Probably. But you know the rules. The new master has to send transport to the halfway house. No one in the organisation ever knows where any of the other members live or who they are. That's a strict rule. All communication is via the satellite link and that's all encoded. I'm sure they've been looking for this place, but they'll never be able to find it.'

'So he saw us both . . .'

'It was my first transfer. I had a Master in Ireland who was a real charmer. He introduced me to it all. I had the time of my life, sure I did. He could make me weep with pleasure . . . Oh, it makes me go all funny inside just to think about the things he did to me . . . But then he told me I had to move, that it was a rule and that they could not make an exception. He made me perform in front of a video camera, made me use a dildo the size of a unicorn horn... I was bought by some fellow in Greece. The Emperor must have seen the transmission. The day I was to be taken from the halfway house – all bound and gagged, and as naked as a spring-born lamb – they pounced.'

'In Greece?'

'Yes. Shipped me over in a fishing boat. Oh, one of the other OIM girls is from Russia. They flew *her* from St Petersburg.'

'My god...'

'I don't think he does it just to get the girls. It's a sort of revenge on the OIM. He wants to try and wreck the organisation. Perhaps he thinks they'll all join up with him.'

Mollie lapsed into silence.

'So what are we going to do?' Melinda whispered.

'Do?'

'We've got to escape.'

Mollie laughed, then clamped her hand over her mouth to stop herself for fear of waking the others.

'Escape!'

'Yes.'

'There's no escape, Melinda.' She pointed to the gold ankle chain and the sapphire. 'That's not for decoration. It's an electronic transmitter. He may be obsessed by ancient Rome, but he's got all the latest gizmos.' She tapped her own ankle where Melinda could see an identical chain and jewel. 'It tags us everywhere we go. The whole villa's surrounded by an invisible electronic net. If one of us steps outside it, the whole place lights up like a Christmas tree.'

'Have you tried?'

'Oh, I was like you when I first arrived. Devoted to

my original Master. I knew he'd be worried about me. Well, I slipped out of the chains in here after a week. They'd forgotten to bolt that door. It was easy. No one was about. I only got as far as the courtyard when all the lights came on. The Nubians caught me. Must have seen me right from the minute I left here. Anyway, I managed to slip out of their grasp. I'm a wriggly little bugger. I just ran for it. As soon as I hit the clearing, there was an alarm that would have woken the dead. They tracked me with a little portable gadget. Didn't get far . . .'

'God.'

'So it's hopeless. And I'll tell you another thing, it's not worth it.'

'What did they do to you?'

Mollie's eyes glazed with tears as she remembered. 'Just don't try to escape.'

'What are we going to do then?'

'We just have to co-operate. He's not bad if you don't cross him. The OIM will find us eventually.'

'Eventually,' Melinda said gloomily.

'There's nothing else we can do, believe me. You just have to pretend he's still one of the Masters, that it's all proper and above board. It's not that bad . . .'

'I've got to escape.'

'Melinda, it's not worth it. Look, I'd better go.' Mollie picked up the hood. 'Sorry,' she said, indicating that she would have to put it back on.

'Can we talk again?'

'Sure we can.' Mollie leant forward and kissed Melinda lightly on the cheek before pulling the soft leather over her head and manoeuvring the gag back into place. Melinda sucked the ball into her mouth and felt the laces being pulled tight, stretching the leather against the contours of her face.

'Don't worry,' Mollie whispered into her ear. 'They will rescue us.'

As she felt Mollie move away, Melinda lay back on the straw palliasse. She was glad that at least she now knew the truth about her situation, but it was deeply depressing. For the moment Mollie was clearly right, there was no alternative but to be the Emperor's willing slave and to behave to him as she would to any of the real Masters. But despite what Mollie had said, she was determined that there must – somewhere or somehow – be a means of escape.

They had allowed her to bathe herself in the big tank. But then Bandu had made her lie flat on one of the stone benches and spread her legs open, so her feet touched the floor on either side. Then she lathered Melinda's sex and pubis, and meticulously shaved away the soft fleece of pubic hair that had grown since she had last been made to shave it away. Kneeling on the bench between her legs, and using, Melinda was relieved to discover, a modern razor, Bandu lathered her twice more to make sure she was completely smooth, pulling her labia this way and that to make sure she got into all her nooks and crannies. When she had finished, she washed away the excess soap and rubbed the whole area with her hand, checking it was completely smooth. She leant back to inspect her work. Every detail of Melinda's sex was visible, the delineation of her inner and outer labia and the little crater of her anus were all perfectly clear. With her legs straddling the bench, the entrance to her vagina was open; Bandu could see that her efforts had made Melinda wet.

Another woman had arrived while this was going on. She came to stand by the bench and looked down at Melinda's labia with studied indifference. Melinda recognised her as the woman who had fixed what she now knew to be the electronic tag to her ankle.

'Dry yourself,' Bandu said, getting to her feet.

Melinda stood up and dried her body thoroughly. The little plump woman had taken two curled gold ornaments from a large wicker bag she had set down on the floor. As soon as Melinda had finished with the towel, she took her hands, one by one, and slid the ornaments up her arms and over her elbows, so they coiled around her flesh. They were designed to look like snakes, the heads inset with jewels to form the eyes and mouth.

The woman took a little palette from the bag. Ordering Melinda to stand still, she sat on the bench and began painting the coils of a snake over one breast and across to the other, a brightly coloured snake with red and green skin. She finished by painting its head to look like it was just about to bite Melinda's left nipple. Transferring her attention to below Melinda's belly, she applied the brush to what was now the clearly visible slit of her sex. Skilfully, she painted the head and part of the body of a large red snake so it seemed to emerge from Melinda's sex.

Two of the Nubians had appeared in the bathhouse as the woman's work was completed. They were carrying some sort of leather harness.

'What is tonight?' the woman said in English, packing away her paints. Her voice had a heavy Italian accent.

'The festival of Juno,' Bandu replied.

'She is ready.'

'Good.'

'She pretty, no?'

'Very,' Bandu agreed, looking at Melinda without her usual air of antipathy.

The woman left as the Nubians dropped the harness by Melinda's feet. They quickly went to work. There was nothing complicated about the arrangement. First they strapped a pair of leather cuffs around Melinda's wrists as she was made to hold them out in front of her. The two cuffs were joined together by a strong metal loop. Then they buckled wide leather straps around her body, at the top of her breasts and around her waist. Further straps followed: on her legs at the top of her thighs, just above the knee and at the ankles. On the outside of each strap there were sturdy metal rings, one on each of the leg straps and two on the ones that ran around her body. They were all carefully positioned so the rings were all in line along the sides of Melinda's body.

'Follow,' Bandu commanded, when the harness was in place.

They all trooped in single file out of the bathhouse and into the courtyard. The moon was low in the sky but was now completely full; the little sliver missing before was now fully visible. The night air was warm. From inside the house, Melinda could hear the babble of conversation, rising occasionally into a crescendo of laughter, then falling back again to more normal levels. An instrument sounding like a lyre played an odd lilting music.

Leaning against the wall – at an entrance to the main house by the swimming pool – was a metal triangle made from tubular steel and well over six feet in length. Set in the steel were loops of metal which Melinda could see opened against a powerful spring.

Bandu stood Melinda in front of the frame and the three other Nubians quickly clipped the loops of metal protruding from the leather straps into the metal spring-loaded rings on the frame. They fixed the final one, the loop between her wrists, to the sharpest angle of the triangle above her head. Melinda was effectively held to the metal frame along the whole of its length. Her torso was fastened to the middle of the triangle and her legs were splayed apart along the edges of the lower half.

They checked that all the springs on the metal rings had closed properly and then, each taking a corner, the Nubian women slowly manoeuvred the triangle and its human cargo into the air at shoulder height, Melinda facing downwards.

They marched through into the house where they came to a halt, after only a few steps, in front of a pair of double doors. There they waited, apparently oblivious to the weight. After perhaps five or six minutes, the lyre stopped playing and Melinda heard a rasping fanfare played on what were clearly primitive brass instruments. The doors were thrown open and the Nubians marched forward. There were cries of delight and applause as they entered. Melinda could see, by turning her head to the side, that they were in yet another marbled room, this time the marble was shaded in soft pinks. Around the room on three sides, were three long, low couches piled with silk cushions in every shape, size and colour. In front of the couches, piled with the debris of what had obviously been a very extensive meal, were three low tables. All the plates and cutlery were gold, as were the chalices that had been used for the wine.

Ten or twelve men and women sat on the couches, the men all in white togas, the women in brightly coloured silk dresses that had obviously been designed in a manner to fit with the Roman theme. Most had a single shoulder-strap, with a diagonal bodice fitting tightly across the breasts and belted at the waist. Most were made from see-through or semi-transparent material.

In front of each woman, on the table among the discarded food, was the unmistakable shape of a phallus, also in gold; perfect replicas of an erect male organ and complete with beautifully sculptured balls. A smaller version had been placed in front of every man.

As two of the overseers by the double doors continued to play a fanfare on oddly shaped brass instruments, Melinda's triangulated body was paraded about the room – first to the table on the left, then to the table on the right – before being brought into the centre, where the Emperor sat in the middle of a couch.

The fanfare ended.

'Friends. Romans . . . may I present to the glory of Juno the latest addition to my little collection, a slave from the province of Britannia.'

There was applause.

'Continue,' he said to Bandu, as a woman on his left in glittering turquoise silk offered him a nectarine, which he bit into like a dog lunging for a bone, showering them both with its juices. He laughed as he tried to eat the rest of the fruit from her palm without using his hands. It fell into her lap and he pursued it there, making her shriek as he snaffled down between her legs. Finally he came up victoriously, the nectarine clamped in his mouth, orange-coloured juice running down his chin into the gold-trimmed toga he was wearing.

As the servants in white tunics scurried about to refill chalices with red wine, the Nubians lowered Melinda and the metal triangle to the ground. There were three pulleys positioned in the centre of the room and hanging from wooden beams, the ropes wound round each tied up to cleats on the side walls.

As soon as Melinda had been rested on the ground, each of the black women went to a cleat and let the ropes down until they were coiled on the floor. Each then came to the frame and tied one of the ropes to the three corners of the metal frame. Back at the cleats they began to haul the metal triangle and Melinda into the air.

Melinda felt a sensation she had never experienced before as her bound body was suspended. The women hauled the apex up higher than the other two corners so her body was slanted and facing the Emperor. She felt a slight jolt as the pulleys were tied up.

The leather belts and metal rings held Melinda firmly, her weight pulling her body against the leather straps. She felt the familiar pulse of excitement that bondage always caused in her body, but it was much stronger than usual as her restraint was so extreme.

None of the guests were eating now, although they were still drinking from the gold chalices. Melinda, from her vantage point above, watched as their bodies began to move closer together and their hands began to explore each other's hidden depths. They did not seem to be paired off in any way, two men groping at one woman, one woman groping at another. All looked at her, their eyes examining her body intently. She recognised the two women who had passed her on the stone column and the fat couple who had come over to her in the courtyard, though they were both now on opposite couches. A man appeared to be pointing out how the snake emerged from Melinda's sex, while one of the women peered at her shaven sex. A male to her right pressed his right hand up under the woman's dress, while his left searched for a way into her bosom.

It was not long before the guests were shedding their clothes. The two men who had been attending the one woman both stood up, discarded their togas at the same time to great claps and cries of approval, thus revealing swollen cocks. A woman rose to pull her dress off, again occasioning applause, and this seemed to be the signal for a more general undressing. But soon there were so many individual acts of disrobing that the crowd did not pay any attention and concentrated instead on each other. Two women caressed each other intimately while a man knelt at their side watching them, his erection in his hand. The two men who had started it all went to work on a woman between them, one having his cock sucked into her mouth, the other dropping between her legs to tongue her sex.

As though responding to some signal, all the guests began to suck or fuck each other. Big erections sank into passages front and rear, while women picked up the dildos. The smaller dildos were reamed into the men's backsides and the larger ones into their own or some other woman's where no male invaded. A woman would frequently find herself penetrated by two different men at the same time, or by a man and a phallus wielded by a woman. A man busily engaged in routing his cock into an awaiting woman would find his own anus invaded, too. It was a Roman orgy, complete in every detail, right down to the waiting Nubians who stood passively, watching the heaving mass of bodies.

The Emperor was still dressed. He got to his feet – having avoided the attentions of the woman in the turquoise dress – and wandered among his guests.

Melinda saw him kneel down to knead the breasts of a woman who was being fucked from behind and then, a little further down the same couch, finger the hairy sex of a woman whose mouth was impaled on a large cock. He allowed another woman to strip off his toga and take his prick in her mouth, but stopped her after a minute or two, pulling her head away by her hair. On the other couch, he stood by the woman who had attracted the attention of two men and watched as she settled herself down on top of one of them, guiding his cock into her sex with her hand, then bending forward so the second man could position himself behind her to push his erection into her smaller passage.

Melinda's body was throbbing as she watched. Everywhere she looked was sex – men and women's bodies joined in every conceivable way, the rhythm of each coupling different, but all with fundamentally the same aim. She felt the leather straps biting into her body and writhed slightly against them. Her legs were not spread far enough apart to stop herself squeezing her clitoris slightly between her thighs. Melinda's eyes settled on the two females who had fallen on each other, heads buried between each other's thighs, mouths working furiously to bring each other off. Melinda felt her clitoris surge as she suddenly remembered Sophia. If she hadn't been abducted, would she be doing exactly the same thing to the beautiful Sophia?

Only the Emperor remained on his feet. He roamed around watching intently – his erection bobbing in front of him – but did not get more than momentarily involved.

Gradually, with so much provocation on every side, the men began to give in to their desire. Melinda watched as buttocks were driven forward faster, mouths fellated more urgently, hands pumped cocks harder, all towards the same end. The first to come was a man kneeling by the two women who were wrapped end to end. His cock had been seized by another woman who knelt behind him, pressing her body into his back while she moved her hand up and down his erection and used one of the small gold dildos in his rear passage. As her hand reached the base of his shaft, and the dildo was pushed to its deepest point, spunk spurted over the two women in front of him, mostly over the back of one, but some landed on the upturned face of the other. It was like a chain reaction. His coming sparked the two women. Their cries and screams of ecstasy proved the final straw for other men, who drove harder into other women and came. Spunk jetted out into the sexes and mouths, and over the body, of the whole writhing, squirming multi-headed monster that the orgy had created.

Only when the last man had come – only when the company relaxed and the coupling was unjoined – did the Emperor give the signal to Bandu and the other Nubians. Melinda felt the metal triangle being lowered. The bottom was lowered to the floor first, so Melinda was almost vertical. As Bandu made sure the rope attached to the top was secured, the other Nubians ran forward and released the ropes from the bottom angles. They guided the triangle backwards as Bandu let out the final rope and the triangle was lowered so Melinda was lying face upwards. Bandu removed the rope and the three Nubians stood back against the walls again, waiting until they were needed.

The women guests reacted immediately. They threw cushions from the couches around Melinda's naked but bound body, then all of them, without exception, jumped over the tables and came to sit or kneel by Melinda's prone and helpless body.

Melinda's excitement was extreme. She knew the Emperor was not a proper Master, and that she should not feel the way she did, but couldn't help herself. After all her months of training as a slave, plus the hoping and praying and longing for a Master to use her in any way he chose – as long as he used *her* in preference to the other slaves – it was inevitable that she should react this way. It was, after all, quite obvious that the Emperor had saved himself for her. He could have had any of the female guests in any combination, but he had waited – remained aloof – despite his throbbing cock. Her Master, waiting for *her*. She tried not to think of him like that and attempted to distance herself. It might have been possible under other circumstances but not now, not after what she had been made to feel, suspended above the crowd. He was her Master, and he was readying himself for her.

As if acting on a secret signal, the women gathered around Melinda's body reached forward in unison. Suddenly there were hands on her breasts and belly and thighs; fingers were pressing up between her labia and buttocks. There were mouths too, kissing and licking and sucking at her flesh, fighting each other for possession of a little scrap of territory, vying with each other to caress or prod or pinch. It reminded Melinda of the way the Nubians had used her in the cubicles of the bathhouse. She felt as if her whole body was alive with sexual sensation.

Hands squeezed and kneaded her breasts, exposing the purple squares where she had been marked. Fingers pinched her nipples, sometimes hard and brutally, sometimes soft and tenderly, both kinds of touch producing equally strong waves of pleasure. She was penetrated front and rear, not by one woman but by two or three; in fact, she could not tell by how many. There was a fierce battle for her clitoris, too many fingers wanting authority over it, but eventually a victor emerged. Melinda felt a relentless tempo beginning – a tapping first, right on the little nut itself, then a more pervasive prodding – someone was pressing her clit down against her pubic bone, then rubbing it from side to side.

It was difficult to keep her eyes open but Melinda tried. She looked at the naked women surrounding her, their breasts jiggling as they worked, nipples all hard, white spunk dried on some of their bodies, eyes alive with excitement. She raised her head to look for the Emperor. The men were on the couches watching intently, but she could not see her Master.

'Here,' he said, knowing what she was looking for. He was standing behind her and, as he spoke, walked forward, placing his feet on either side of the triangle to which she was still bound.

Melinda arched her head back and looked up his legs. His big balls and cock looked even larger in this position, his ball sac hanging down like some ripe fruit, his cock sticking out at a right angle to his torso.

'Oh please, Master . . .' she begged, knowing it was breaking the rules but too excited to control herself.

'I am your Master,' he said.

'Yes. Yes, Master.'

As she watched, she saw him kneel, descending on her until his balls were resting against her cheek.

'Lick me, child. Make your Master happy.' His normally high-pitched voice was made husky by his need.

She obeyed immediately, feeling her own body beginning to quiver with excitement. The hands and mouths all over her seemed no longer to be individual: it was as if they were all one, belonging to the same animal, a huge multi-limbed, multi-headed monster. They worked in harmony – the caressing and kneading hands, the sucking wet mouths, the penetrating fingers all joined. The women began to caress each other, too. Hands that could find no room on Melinda's body strayed to the breast of their nearest neighbour, or slid over a buttock, delving below to test the wetness there. Mouths also met over Melinda's body, forming an arch of female flesh.

It did not disturb the rhythm. In fact, it made it stronger. The more the women were linked, the more they touched and held and caressed, the greater the pleasure they generated, the mass of bodies cranking up the voltage of an electric charge.

Melinda bucked her body against the leather that held her so firmly, wanting to feel its constraint. She tried to concentrate on sucking and licking at her Master's balls but it was almost impossible. Her body was starting to come, the engine of the motor that drove her to orgasm already humming loudly. She wanted to hold out, let his spunk take her over the edge, but she knew she couldn't do it. She fought the waves of feeling that flooded over her but they were too strong. She let herself go, giving in, allowing herself to be swept away and instantly feeling the muscles of her body lock, her tendons pulling against the straps that held them so securely. Her nerves were overwhelmed with an explosion of sensation created by the writhing octopus of women's hands and mouths around and inside her. Her cry of ecstasy was stifled by the Master's balls.

The Emperor got to his feet. The women melted away. After being surrounded by so much body heat, Melinda now felt a chill. She opened her eyes. The Emperor was standing at the side of her now, looking down at her body. One of the women stood behind him. She looked triumphant, the chosen one. Everyone else in the room watched intently. The woman was dark, big breasted, her buttocks round and generous, her thighs broad. She was holding one of the small gold phalluses in her hand, which she licked, covering it with a film of saliva, then plugged it into the Emperor's anus while her other hand slid around his hips to grasp his cock.

Melinda saw him shudder at her first touch. There was a trail of fluid leaking from his urethra. It wasn't going to take long. The woman rubbed her finger over the ridge at the bottom of the glans, using his own juice for lubrication.

The gold phallus pumped in and out. The woman pressed her breasts into his shoulder-blades.

Melinda saw his cock throb and swell. She should have felt jealous but she didn't. Instead she felt honoured. The Emperor was looking straight into her jade-green eyes, his gaze unwavering. It was as though he could see into her soul and was doing all this just for her. As his cock jerked, as his spunk arced out of him and splashed down on her belly and breasts, she knew it was for *her* and nobody else.

Six

Melinda lay on the straw palliasse in the dormitory. As usual, she was chained to the floor by her wrist, the tight leather helmet was laced around her head and pressing the gag into her mouth. It was the third night since the orgy occasioned by the Festival of Juno and neither she nor any of the other body slaves had been called to serve the Emperor.

She had had lots of time to consider everything that had happened and to digest the information Mollie had given her, but time had not made things appear any more simple. She was as confused now as she had been at the moment when she was first kidnapped.

After her unfortunate experience in Paris, all she had wanted to do was re-establish herself – in her own eyes as much as in the eyes of the OIM – as the perfect slave, a model of submission and obedience. Seeing Sophia at the halfway house had made her excitement at the prospect seem even more pronounced.

Now a different sort of eagerness dominated her emotions. There was no doubt that what had happened since her arrival at the villa was as extreme as anything she had experienced with her previous Masters. She only had to think of being bound to the metal triangle and suspended in mid-air, then lowered and handled so outrageously, to make herself almost dizzy with rapture, her sex throbbing instantly. Not to mention the explosive orgasm she had finally been allowed in the cellars at the end of the test or what the Nubians had done to her. It was, of course, difficult not to think of these things. As she lay awake in the enforced darkness of the leather hood, her mind seemed to become like a video screen, playing and replaying the images it had so recently absorbed.

But the more she thought about it and revelled in it, the more she felt guilty. The way the Emperor had treated her at the dinner, the way he had saved himself for her – *her* above all the other beautiful women he could have used – was thrilling because she had thought of him as her Master. But he was not. He was not a Master at all. He was not entitled to her respect and he was certainly not entitled to her obedience. Her allegiance was to the OIM and to her original Master, Walter Hammerton. She had no right to treat the Emperor as she had sworn to treat the other Masters. In doing so she felt she was betraying them, but particularly the man who had opened up the doors of her sexual imagination and given her the opportunity for a life beyond her wildest dreams.

But what could she do? On the one hand she wished she could find a means of escape. On the other, the Emperor was bewitching her. She knew she must not allow herself to come under his spell but it was impossible. As long as she was at the villa, his effect on her would be the same and her excitement – however guilty – would be unabated. The only way to escape it was to escape the villa. The total lack of any way to measure the passage of time – like the absence of mirrors – shaped Melinda's life. She had learnt to accept that it was no longer her concern. Time was something only her Master was privy to. Her time belonged to her Master; it was not for her to know how long he wished to keep her waiting. Like everything else in her life, it depended on him.

She did not know how long, therefore, she had lain on the lumpy straw mattress before she heard the dormitory door open again. No more than an hour seemed to have passed since the Nubians had hooded and chained up all the slaves. Now they marched into the room and Melinda heard the rattle of chains as manacles were unlocked. She felt the heat of a body kneeling next to her, and fingers soon freed the manacle on her wrist and pulled her into a sitting position. The laces at the back of the hood were freed less quickly, but eventually the leather was pulled from Melinda's head.

As she looked around, she saw that each of the four Nubians – their bodies clad in the usual leather skirts like Roman centurions and tight halter tops – had unchained a body slave. In a little procession they were led out of the dormitory, along the marbled corridors of the main building and – for the first time in Melinda's case – upstairs. At the top of a straight flight of stairs they were led down a much narrower corridor than the ones on the ground floor, off which was a series of doors. The Nubians guided the four selected slaves through one of the smallest of these doors, beyond which was a medium-sized room with a heavily curtained window.

The room was furnished like a bedroom, although all the furniture was in the Roman style, or could at least pass as such at a glance. There was a double bed with scrolled head- and footboards, on which four neat piles of clothes had been lain.

'Put these on quick,' Bandu said, her voice lowered to a whisper. The slaves had all been led to stand in front of a particular pile, each matched, presumably, to their size.

Melinda picked up the first item. It was a blue satin halter top, no bigger than a bra. Under it was a pair of chiffon pantaloons with a matching blue satin waistband and cuffs around the ankles. She put the top on first. It was a little small for her, and her breasts spilled over the satin cups. As she pulled the baggy trousers over her hips, she discovered they had no crotch, the chiffon on the inside ending at the top of her thigh. There was a small pair of slippers, in the same blue satin, which fitted her feet perfectly.

The other three slaves had identical costumes, though the colour of the satin of each was different – one a bright yellow, another a dark purple and the last a deep red. Together they looked like a scene from the Arabian nights.

Melinda looked at their faces but did not recognise any of them. They were not the body slaves she had seen serving the Emperor before, though they were all beautiful. They had been chosen, she guessed, for contrast. One was a tall redhead, another a petite long-haired blonde; there was a brunette, whose figure was fuller than any of the others and her, of course – a tall and short-haired flaxen blonde.

As soon as the body slaves were dressed, Bandu indicated to the redhead, who was standing nearest to her, that she should follow her out of the room. Another Nubian followed her also.

The door closed after them; the other three waited, not knowing what to expect next. Melinda's heart was pounding. She hoped they were there to serve the Master and were being taken to his bedroom. Her excitement, as it had before, overcame her misgivings.

It was a few minutes before Bandu returned. She picked another of the harem, this time the full-figured brunette, and led her away. After an equal space of time the petite blonde was also taken away, leaving Melinda alone. Did this mean she was intended for something different from the other three? In her fevered imagination, such speculations arose only too easily.

Bandu returned and indicated for Melinda to follow her. They went back down the corridor to the very end, where two imposing doors were framed by caryatid pillars. Each panel on the doors was carved with a relief of what looked like scenes of Roman military victories. In one, for example, Roman centurions in massed ranks – shields raised and knitted together in a make-shift barrier – were fighting off the disorganised rabble of Celts or Gauls or Huns.

Bandu pushed one of the doors open and led Melinda forward. This was clearly the Emperor's bedroom. The walls were hung with yards and yards of sheer silk, which rustled slightly from the draught from the door. A curtain of silk hung down the centre of the room, too, and it was not until Bandu parted it that Melinda saw the bed, and the other three slaves.

The bed was long and wide, not pushed against a wall but set in the middle of the floor. It was covered in silk sheets and a profusion of white cushions. At each of its corners, though not actually part of the frame of the bed, was a stone pillar runing from floor to ceiling. Each of the three body slaves had been bound to one of the pillars, facing in towards the bed, their feet resting on the corner of the frame that supported the mattress. Their hands were tied to a metal ring set into the stone above their heads, their ankles bound to the base of the column by a single rope. The knots at their wrists and ankles were arranged in such a way that they could be quickly released by pulling on a slip-knot.

Bandu took Melinda to the vacant pillar, made her stand on the frame of the bed and, with the help of the other Nubian, quickly bound her into position using the same arrangement of knots. Then she produced a small torpedo-shaped object no bigger than the top of a pen. Pushing Melinda's thighs apart slightly, she inserted the object into her shaven labia, which closed over it, concealing it from view.

Melinda immediately felt her sex react. The end of the little cylinder was positioned in such a way as to rub against her clitoris. By the look on the faces of all the other body slaves, the same device had been applied to them.

'You not let it out,' Bandu warned. The two black women swept back through the silk curtaining that divided the room, then Melinda heard the heavy door close.

Simultaneously, another door on the other side of the room opened and the Emperor walked in. He was accompanied by a male overseer in the ubiquitous white tunic. The Emperor was rubbing his wet hair with a towel. A loose, multicoloured robe hung from his shoulders. When he reached the bed, he handed the towel to the overseer and allowed him to strip the robe away, leaving the Emperor naked. The overseer parted the silk curtain and went out through the main door.

'Very pretty,' the Emperor said, as he climbed on to the bed, his big, fleshy frame trembling slightly as he moved. He positioned a cushion under his head and pulled a sheet up over his body. He was facing

Melinda, who was on his left side. Looking at the slaves one by one, he smiled. 'You're the lucky ones tonight. Aren't you?'

Four voices all answered, 'Yes, master.'

'I should have had you all whipped first by the Nubians. That would get those tight little buttocks squirming a bit, and your tits. Life's too easy for you. Much too easy.' He closed his eyes. 'You must be very quiet . . .' he said, without opening them again. 'Very quiet. You are here in case I wake and wish to indulge myself. Sometimes I do and sometimes I don't.' He smiled. 'Just make sure you don't make a sound, or tomorrow you will be providing entertainment for my guests.'

The lighting in the room was soft and concealed, but definitely electric. Melinda saw the Emperor's hand move out of the sheet and press a small switch on the side of the frame above his head. The room was plunged into darkness. Only a few minutes later, the Emperor's breathing had changed and he was clearly asleep.

The object between Melinda's labia could only be kept in place if she held her thighs together. Unfortunately, this also had the effect of pressing it against her clitoris. She knew why it had been placed there. The pressure on her clitoris, the feeling of the hard little cylinder buried in her labia, was making her sex wet. She could feel it. If the Emperor woke and wanted to use one of the body slaves, they would be ready for him, not just mentally but physically too. She concentrated on holding the cylinder firmly in place, and on what it was doing to her sex. The tip of the cylinder seemed to be alive, though she knew that was only her imagination. It seemed to be probing her clitoris, touching and teasing it. The longer the cylinder stayed in place, the more her imagination seized the opportunity to magnify its effect on her.

Sleep was going to be impossible. Very little light filtered through the big windows of the room, which were covered in the same material as the walls. Occasionally, the moon must have come out from a covering of cloud, because the room was suddenly bathed in grey ghostly light, but mostly it was difficult to see across to the far wall. Melinda could see the other women's eyes – and the sparkle of excitement that danced in them like flames in a fire – as they experienced the same provocations that raced through her own body.

As much as she tried to tell herself it should not be the case, it was the thought of the Emperor waking – of untying the two slip-knots and hauling her down on to the bed that thrilled her most. She tried not to think of him as her Master, that he did not matter to her in the way Walter or the Countess had mattered, but it was impossible. He behaved like a Master, had the power and authority and hypnotic quality of a Master, knew how to treat her and enthral her, like she was *his* slave. That was what made it impossible for Melinda to dismiss him as a normal man and to disobey him. She was, at least for now, *his* slave; the thought had such a powerful resonance in her body and mind that it was impossible to ignore, which was just as well, as it might be a long time before she found any means of escape.

Time passed slowly. In the gloom, she tried to look at the bodies of the other three slaves. The longhaired blonde was immediately opposite her, hair falling over one shoulder and partially obstructing the yellow satin halter that held her big breasts so tightly. Despite being the shortest of the four women, her breasts were the biggest, balloons of flesh crushed together by the material into a long deep cleavage. Below the halter, her naked belly was flat and Melinda could see that she, too, had been shaved. She could also see, when flashes of moonlight permitted, that she was holding her thighs together exactly as Melinda was, to keep the cylinder in place – not only for fear of punishment but because she wanted to be ready in case the Emperor woke up.

Melinda could not see the redhead or the brunette as clearly, but from what she could make out, it was obvious their feelings were the same. All four body slaves shared the same motivation, hoping the Emperor would wake to pick them, imagining the ropes falling away as they were pulled down to serve their Master. Each dreaded having to watch as one of the others was used in preference to them. Like Melinda, they all sent silent messages to him, subtly angling their bodies towards him and preparing themselves for what might never come.

Eventually, the passion and anxiety took its toll. Melinda felt herself beginning to doze, but she didn't sleep for long. Her head would fall forward jerking her arms against the rope, which would wake her again. If she jammed her head back between her arms, she could prevent this to some extent and sleep for longer periods, though she was worried her thighs might part and her labia yield their secret treasure.

She had, she thought, been asleep for some time when a noise woke her. She opened her eyes to see the Emperor throwing back the sheet, his cock erect. He was looking up, above his head, at the petite blonde. Reaching out with his hand, he pulled the slip-knot on her ankles. Crawling backwards on the bed, he positioned his head at her feet and looked up her legs into her shaven sex. He used one hand to part her legs and with the other he deftly caught the little cylinder as it fell from her labia. He brought it up to his mouth and sucked it.

'Mmm . . .' he murmured.

Getting to his feet, he then released the slip-knot on the blonde's wrists. She collapsed forward on to the bed, her muscles useless after being constricted for so long. As her circulation returned, he reached for the switch and turned on the lights. They came on as dimly as before.

The Emperor lay on his back again and pushed the blonde's head into his lap. He did not need to tell her what to do. She knelt between his legs and wrapped her lips around his cock. Melinda watched as she dropped her head down onto it, swallowing the whole thick shaft. The Emperor moaned. Immediately the blonde woman pulled her head away, his cock appeared, painted with her saliva, only to disappear again as she drove her head forward, glad of the opportunity to display her skills.

The three other body slaves watched intently, hoping against hope that this was perhaps only a preliminary, that the Emperor would choose again, or, at the very least, want another slave to join in. As the blonde fellated him so comprehensively Melinda saw his eyes looking at her, and for a moment she thought he was about to untie her. Then his eyes flicked to the redhead and her heart sunk as rapidly as it had risen.

The blonde slave's long hair swept over the Emperor's thighs as her head bobbed up and down. Melinda could see the little cylinder lying on the silk sheet where the Emperor had dropped it, no longer needed to keep the body slave wet and primed. His own cock was doing that job now. Melinda felt a strong pang of jealousy. Why hadn't the Master chosen her?

Without a word, the Emperor gripped the woman's head. He pulled her up towards him, making her straddle his hips, raised on her haunches, but held her up so she did not descend on to his cock.

Melinda could see his glistening erection nestling into the blonde woman's smooth, hairless labia as the Emperor positioned her over it. Her buttocks were as fleshy as her breasts and seemed to be trembling in anticipation under the billowing chiffon of the strange pantaloons. She reached behind her back and freed the satin halter that held her breasts – whether at her own instigation or the Emperor's, Melinda could not tell. As she threw the garment aside, she shook her shoulders from side to side and her breasts slapped into each other as they gyrated. Then she caught them in her hand and proudly, like someone performing their favourite party trick, fed first her left nipple into her mouth and then her right, taking them each between her teeth and baring her lips so the Emperor could see her puckered flesh being bitten hard. Under her breasts, Melinda glimpsed the purple squares that indicated that she too belonged to the OIM.

It was only when she finally released her right nipple – the marks of her teeth clearly visible on it, her big breast falling back on to her chest – that the Emperor pulled her down on to him and his cock slid past her labia into the heat and wetness that had been waiting for so long for him. She sunk down deep, wriggling her bottom to get him as far up as he would go and squashing her clitoris against his pubic bone.

'Oh, Master...' she gasped.

She rode him like a horse, up and down on the

saddle of his lap, impaling herself on him, letting him feel how wet she was and how much she wanted him, her breasts jumping up and down on her chest.

'Oh, Master, Master.'

She rode faster and faster, the chiffon pantaloons no obstruction to her endeavours. He did nothing to discourage her. She shook her head from side to side, her blonde hair flowed out as though it were blowing in the wind.

Melinda's body was rigid, her muscles taut. She watched every movement, at the same time wishing she could see nothing. How long the Emperor had been a member of the organisation she did not know, but he certainly knew the ways of the Masters. This was simultaneous torture and tease. Torture to watch another slave having such intimate pleasure with a Master, who had ignored *her* and favoured this girl instead; tease because Melinda could feel his cock ramming into *her*, could feel her own wetness running down his shaft, her clit jammed between their bodies. Her whole body was pulsing as her imagination ran riot.

She watched her Master's face. He had his head thrown to one side, his cheek pressing down on the silk sheet. His hips were moving in time to the body slave's furious tempo. It was obvious from the locked muscles that lined his face that he was going to let her make him come.

Suddenly, he moved his head and looked straight into Melinda's eyes, just as he had on the night of the dinner. The impact was so great, his eyes so powerful and charismatic, that she felt as though he were touching her. His expression was inquiring, searching; he wanted to know her feelings, how she felt about this spectacle. His eyes did not move away this time, but held firm. Even in the dim light Melinda could see how they changed, how he recognised her excitement and, feeding off it, increased his own desire.

He reached forward and grabbed the blonde body slave by both hips, forcing her down on him and making her stay down. But despite this, his eyes never left Melinda, not looking at the slave with whom he was joined, watching Melinda instead. She could see his eyes roaming her body as he pressed his cock into the cavern of the other woman's sex. He looked at Melinda's breasts in the blue satin halter, at her hourglass waist and naked belly, and at the chiffon that veiled her contoured thighs. His eyes narrowed as he stared at the apex of her thighs and the hairless triangle that revealed the first inch of the furrow of her labia beyond which the little cylinder was neatly buried.

Melinda angled herself towards him. Her eyes tried to tell him how much she wanted and desired him, how much her body throbbed for his attentions. It was true; all her reservations and the complications of her situation were thrust aside. She had never wanted a man more, never wanted to serve a Master as much or as completely.

He looked up again, straight into her eyes. His hands pulled the body slave down on him another fraction of an inch. Then, for a moment Melinda felt – yet again – as though they were touching, as though they were joined together by something much more powerful than a physical pull. The connection was broken as his eyes rolled upwards and she saw the icy blue replaced by the whites of his eyes. Then the eyelids closed, squeezed tightly shut by the same convulsion that rocked every other muscle in his body, as he shot hot spunk into the pliant, wet sex of his body slave.

'Master,' she cried, as she felt his orgasm inside her.

'Master,' Melinda echoed. She felt it clearly and distinctly, as if she, too, had been penetrated.

It seemed a long time before the Emperor opened his eyes again. But when he did, he was still looking straight at Melinda. His expression had changed again; now it was taunting, cruel and hard. He enjoyed her discomfort and his power, but Melinda did not mind. He had given her more than he had the long-haired blonde. The Emperor had presented her with his spunk, but Melinda had had his mind. He had come in the sex of one woman, but in his mind he had come for *her*.

There appeared to be no routine at the villa, at least not in the lives of the Emperor's body slaves. They were woken together by the Nubians and their hoods and manacles removed. Then they were marched to the bathhouse, where they used the big tank four at a time. At night they were all hooded and chained.

Apart from this, Melinda never had any idea what would happen next or when. Mollie had visited her twice in the week that had passed since the evening spent in the Emperor's bedroom. She had told her that body slaves were rarely used for domestic chores – as they both had been at their previous establishments – and were kept purely to satisfy the Emperor's personal whims. Occasionally, she told her, a special guest would arrive and the Emperor would allow him or her to use the body slaves as they saw fit, but that was rare. The Emperor preferred to keep the body slaves for himself, leaving his guests to pick from the working slaves. He did not care particularly what they did when their services were not required.

The Nubians arranged for them to take exercise,

and gave them access to a library that had an extensive collection of books on Greco-Roman culture and history, but which stopped after the Sack of Rome in AD 455. The rest of the day was spent either in the dormitory awaiting the Emperor's pleasure or in grooming. The slaves were expected to work on each other's hair and nails and other personal chores to keep them looking spruce. Such activities were strictly supervised, however, and talking was definitely not allowed.

Food was served in the dormitory twice a day – in the mornings after the bathhouse routine, and at dusk. It was after the evening meal and before the body slaves were usually bedded down that Bandu strode purposefully through the door and headed directly for Melinda.

'Follow me,' she said, in her rich, dark voice.

The big black woman, the tongues of the leather skirt slapping up and down against her thighs as she moved, led the way into the bathhouse. She ordered Melinda to bathe and then laid her on the stone bench to shave her pubis once again, although it had only been done the day before and had hardly had a chance to regrow. Washing the soap away, she left Melinda lying on the cold stone while she massaged her body with a sweetly scented body oil. She smoothed the unguent into every inch of her skin, from the tips of her toes to the ends of her fingers, her strong hands kneading it in. Bandu paid special attention to Melinda's firm, round breasts and her thighs, then got her to turn over and salvered the oil over her buttocks, parting them with her hands to make sure the oil penetrated between.

Making Melinda sit up, the black woman picked up some little earthenware pots and brushed

Melinda's eyes with their contents. They could have been some ancient formula, but Melinda suspected that their origin was a little more prosaic. Bandu applied eye-liner and shadow and a bright red lipstick. As usual, no mirror was provided for Melinda to see the results of Bandu's handiwork.

'Put on,' she said, as she held up a long white robe with a single shoulder-strap and tight diagonal bodice. Melinda pulled it over her body, the sensation of being clothed again – as when she had worn the toga the first time she had been presented to the Emperor, after so long naked – not mitigated by the fact that the material of the dress was semi-transparent. The silky material rubbed against her body in a way she had never been aware of when she wore clothes every day, every movement she made producing a new sensation. Her flesh seemed to have become incredibly sensitive, and her nipples grew instantly erect.

'Follow,' Bandu ordered.

They walked into the cool marble corridors of the main house. In the large hall with the platform at one end, Melinda glimpsed a group of guests taking it in turns to whip a naked girl suspended by her wrists from long chains hanging down from the ceiling. Judging by the red weals already evident on her buttocks she had been there for some time. But the throne was empty. The game was obviously not of the Emperor's devising, or perhaps it was just too simple for his tastes.

Melinda hoped she was being taken to the Master. None of the slaves had been summoned during the week, nor had the Emperor been seen about the house. Perhaps he had been away and had just returned. Perhaps the look they had shared, the mental bond they had forged, was about to be turned into a more corporeal attachment.

They mounted the stairs and went down the corridor towards the Master's bedroom, Melinda's heart beating faster as it approached. But Bandu stopped her two doors away. She opened a single door on the right-hand side and indicated for Melinda to enter.

The light in the room was dim. The sun had set while they were in the bathhouse and long shadows of twilight were cast across the room from the large window that overlooked the atrium. Like the Master's bedroom, the walls were lined with a gauzy billowing silk and a large bed was placed in the centre of the room. The bed was also surrounded by the same sort of gauze as the walls, a tent of material hanging down from a single point in the ceiling directly over the centre of the bed.

Bandu led Melinda over to the bed. As far as she could tell, the room was deserted. The two women waited, Bandu's black body difficult to discern in the fading light.

Melinda heard water running. There was another door at the far end of the room and after a few minutes it opened. A young man entered, who, as he came closer, looked no more than a boy. His hair was dark and very curly, and he had serious-looking brown eyes and a gaunt thin face with hollow cheekbones. He was wearing a cotton robe, the first obviously modern garment Melinda had seen since she had arrived at the villa. His body was slender and the areas of flesh that the loose robe revealed were covered in thick black hair. What muscles Melinda could see looked strong and athletic.

'Sir,' Bandu said.

'She is beautiful,' he said, looking Melinda up and

down earnestly. His English had only the slightest trace of an Italian accent.

'She will obey.'

'Obey?' He looked deeply perplexed.

'Whatever you command.'

The boy parted the curtaining around the bed and sat on the thick mattress, which was covered in a pale-blue silk sheet.

'Would you like that I stay, too?' Bandu asked, smiling, her big white teeth shining like lights in the gloom.

'Stay?' The boy seemed terribly uneasy, as if he didn't really know what to do or say.

'It is permitted.'

'You mean . . .'

'We, together.' She made a gesture which included Melinda.

Far from being excited at the thought, the boy looked scared. 'No . . . no . . .' he said quickly. 'I mean, I don't think . . .' He ran out of words.

Bandu looked disappointed, though Melinda could not imagine exactly why. 'I go then.' She strode to the door. 'If you have special needs . . .' She pointed to a large chest standing against one wall – its panels carved with reliefs of what looked like Roman orgies and it's lid tent-shaped – then opened the door and closed it sharply behind her.

The boy got to his feet as soon as they were alone. He went to a small concealed switch by the door and turned it on. The room was lit by the same sort of diffuse light that Melinda had seen in the Emperor's bedroom. 'It sounded like a good idea. Now I'm not so sure,' he said, his perplexity quite obvious. Melinda remained silent. Even if she had been prepared to break the rules, she could think of nothing to say.

The boy looked at her. 'You're really gorgeous.' Very tentatively, he raised his hand and touched her cheek. 'As soft as silk.'

He appeared in two minds; about to send her away on one hand, but intrigued and attracted to her on the other. 'You will do anything I say. Is that true?'

'Yes, Master.' Although initially disappointed that she had not been brought to the Emperor's bedroom, Melinda began to feel a certain excitement. The boy was handsome enough and certainly strong and fit. But there was something else about him, something vaguely familiar that Melinda could not quite put her finger on.

'Anything?' he repeated.

'Yes, Master.'

Curiosity began to get the better of him. 'Kneel,' he said, experimentally.

Melinda got to her knees. The floor of the bedroom was wooden, but there was a thick rug by the bed where she knelt.

'Up,' the boy said, smiling almost in disbelief as Melinda got to her feet again. His smile turned into a grin.

He pushed back the silk drapes around the bed and sat in front of her.

'You're trained for this?'

'Yes, Master.'

'You want to do it?'

'Yes, Master.'

He was shaking his head from side to side; amusement turned to amazement. 'I mean, he told me but I just didn't believe it. It's unbelievable.' His tone changed suddenly. 'Undo my robe,' he said, with a voice of authority, as if testing a role to see whether he could play it.

Melinda leant forward and pulled the knotted cotton belt that held his robe in place. The folds of the garment fell away to reveal his legs and belly, his cock sitting on his thighs amongst a mass of curly black hair. It was beginning to engorge slightly.

'Now take your dress off.' He tried to keep his voice steady – as though ordering a woman to undress was something he did every day, like asking for a cup of coffee – but a certain croakiness gave his excitement away.

Melinda slipped down the single shoulder-strap and released the hooks that held the tight bodice in place. The white silk cascaded to the floor. The boy stared up at Melinda's voluptuous body. He blushed a deep red.

'I thought . . .' he muttered, 'I thought you'd be wearing . . . you know . . . panties and things . . .' Her nakedness under the dress had taken him by surprise. He blushed an even deeper crimson when he noticed her shaven sex and the pronounced pout of her labia between the very top of her thighs.

She sensed that he was on the point of sending her away, fear overcoming the bravado he had initially displayed. But as his eyes roamed her body – as she saw him taking in her high, round breasts, her big nipples, the flare of her hips from her narrow waist, then staring fixedly at her shaven pubis, as though it was the first time he had ever seen such a thing – the blush drained away and she saw his cock pulse.

'I've been away at school in England for the last three years,' he said quietly. 'I had no idea about all this . . .' His eyes swept around the room. 'Before, I was never allowed to come to this house. But my father decided it was time.'

His father! *That* was what Melinda recognised in

him. There was a distinct family resemblance, though the eyes, of course, were a different colour. This boy's father was undoubtedly the Emperor.

'He wanted me to see all that he had built. All this will be mine one day, so he said. And a lot more besides...' he said, wistfully. Still sitting on the bed, he extended his hand as tentatively as before, to touch her thigh just above the knee. 'So soft,' he said, pressing his fingers between her legs. 'What's your name?'

'Melinda, Master.'

'I'm Hadrian, named after the Emperor, of course. Anyway, you can see it's a bit daunting for me, a bit overwhelming... all this... To tell you the truth I'm not sure I want it...' He was talking to her like a friend, not a slave. That made Melinda uneasy, as she was not sure how she was meant to respond.

'How long have you been here?'

'Two weeks, Master.'

'Not long. But you *have* been with other Masters?'

'Yes, Master.'

'All over the world?'

'Yes, Master.'

'My father says there is a big organisation. But he doesn't approve ... says he's got plans of his own...' His eyes were looking at Melinda's body again. 'Step out of the dress,' he ordered, more confidently this time.

Melinda stepped clear of the circle of white silk.

'Pick it up.'

She stooped to do as she was told. He indicated a small wooden bench and she put the dress over it, then came back to stand in front of him.

'Must keep everything neat.'

This time his hand was not at all tentative. He

reached out and stroked her belly. 'I knew nothing about this. Nothing. And now I discover ...' he searched for the right words, '... a whole new world. This really is like ancient Rome, isn't it?'

'Yes, Master.'

'Complete with slaves, real live slaves.'

Stroking her belly had given him an erection. He had a long but not particularly fat cock. It was circumcised, and a dribble of fluid had leaked from his urethra. It was as hairy as the rest of his body, only the top half of his cock smooth and hairless.

'Kneel ...' he said, again with much more authority. 'Kneel, slave.'

Melinda knelt in front of him.

'Will you suck my cock?' he asked, not looking her in the eye, his voice strangulated by his excitement. Clearly he was still finding it difficult to comprehend the situation.

'Yes, Master,' she replied at once. She was finding the situation more and more exciting. It was obvious this was the first time the boy had been exposed to any of the slaves; the idea that the Emperor had selected her for his son's first experience was thrilling. The feeling they had shared when their eyes had met had borne fruit after all.

She pushed between Hadrian's legs and dipped her head forward, letting him see her tongue eagerly lick up the fluid that had leaked from his cock. His body shuddered at the touch. Gently, she eased forward, pursing her lips around his pink glans and sucking it into her mouth. She felt it throbbing.

'I *can* fuck you, can't I?' he said, almost in disbelief. The crudity made his cock spasm.

'Yes, Master,' she said, without taking his cock from her mouth, her tongue and lips forming the words around it. His prick spasmed once again.

Melinda sunk her mouth down deeper as she flicked her tongue along the length of his shaft. She felt the tip of his cock nudging into her throat, and heard the boy moan loudly.

'Don't . . .' he said suddenly, seizing her head in both hands. His cock was throbbing wildly.

Melinda knew what was going to happen. She tried to open her mouth to relieve the pressure but it was too late. His sexual experience was very limited. He had never had a woman use her mouth on him, and certainly never a beautiful, naked woman who was at his every command.

'No . . .' he cried, as he felt his spunk shoot out of his cock and into the wet, warm confines of her mouth and throat. There was so much of it, jetting out at first and striking her with real force, then spattering more gently. Melinda thought she was going to choke.

The instant it was over, he pulled his cock away and got to his feet, blushing vividly again. He dived into the bathroom and slammed the door behind him, his embarrassment complete.

Melinda used the sheet to wipe away a trickle of spunk that had escaped from the corner of her mouth. She had experienced a young boy before when she had been in Spain. It was a shock, naturally enough, for a boy who had previously had to use cunning and guile in an attempt to seduce a woman – and may well have failed – suddenly to be faced with a woman who would do whatever he asked without question, no seduction necessary.

Hadrian had been thrown in at the deep end by his father. He had had no warning and no time to prepare himself. Not that his embarrassment was a problem for Melinda. In fact, it occurred to her, it might be a considerable advantage. She had the feeling that if she could ingratiate herself with Hadrian, gain his confidence, he might be very useful to her – very useful indeed. But she wasn't at all sure how.

Stealing herself to act independently, for once, to do something she had not been told to do, she got up and walked to the bathroom door. It was hard to break her training, more so than she would have imagined, but it was necessary. She tapped on the door lightly.

'Master . . .' she began, again finding it hard to speak without being spoken to first.

She heard water running and then being turned off. The bathroom door opened and Hadrian emerged with a pale blue towel wrapped around his waist. 'You may go,' he said brusquely, not looking her in the eye. 'I'm sorry . . .' he started to say, then stopped. 'I didn't mean to . . .' That sentence ran out of words, too.

'Master . . .' Melinda's heart was pounding. The habit of not speaking until she was asked a question was so engrained in her that it felt completely wrong to break it. She expected someone to burst through the door at any moment having discovered her crime. 'It's all right . . .' she continued falteringly. 'Please . . . just let me . . .'

Melinda extended her hand. She touched his shoulder and slid her hand down his hairy chest to his nipple; she felt his body thrill as she touched it.

'Don't make me go,' she said, looking into his dark brown eyes. 'Please.'

'I don't think I can . . .'

'Sh . . .' she said, putting her finger to his lips, then tracing it over them. 'All you have to do is watch.'

She could see he was undecided. He wanted her,

the cause of his embarrassment, removed. But, at the same time, he felt he might like to explore the renewed desire he had experienced, unexpectedly, as she had tweaked his nipple.

Melinda took the initiative. She took his hand and led him to the bed, thankful he did not pull away. Parting the gauzy drapes, she knelt on the bed and pulled him after her, readjusting the silk so it fell back into place, cocooning them inside. She felt like a spider trapping a fly in her gossamer web.

Hadrian still looked apprehensive, as though he was about to change his mind. 'Look, I think I should . . .'

'Please, Master . . . Just watch me.'

She crawled up the big bed and lay on her back, her feet almost touching his knees. Very slowly and deliberately, she scissored her legs open as wide as they would go, exposing her hairless sex. She bent her legs and angled her sex up at him so he could also see the bud of her anus, her corrugated flesh forming a neat and near-perfect circle.

She could see him studying her intently, and guessed that he had never seen a woman quite as intimately before. With the tips of the fingers on both hands, she held her labia apart so he could see the little bud of her clitoris, pink and wet. Then, with one finger, she began rubbing and tracing circles around it. She moaned involuntarily and felt her sex moisten with her juices.

'It's beautiful,' he said.

'Yes, Master.'

His indecision disappeared along with his flaccidity, and Melinda saw his cock beginning to swell. She left her sex and turned her attention to her tits, taking them in her hands and massaging them aggressively.

Then she took her nipples between her thumb and forefinger and pulled up her breasts, revealing the purple marks on the underside.

'What are they?' he asked, tearing his eyes away from her sex.

'My marks, Master. To show that I am a willing slave.'

The words made his cock surge. Something about the marks excited him, as though they confirmed that the world he had been thrown into wasn't just some crazy dream. He circled his erection with his hand. His cock was as hard as it had been before. He felt a surge of pride.

'Oh, Master, see how wet you've made me?' Melinda said, knowing her open sex would be glistening with her juices.

'Yes.'

'You see, Master,' she said, looking at his cock. 'You see, you're ready again. Don't send me away.' She knew she was safe saying that now.

'No, I won't. You're so beautiful, Melinda.'

He squeezed his cock in his fist as she arched her body off the bed, kneading the pliant flesh of her breasts so they spilt through her fingers like soft dough.

Melinda raised her head to look straight into his eyes, which she could see were full of passion and excitement. She had achieved her objective. She moved her foot, wriggling down the bed so she could reach his cock. Pushing her toes against his hand, he unravelled the grip on his cock so she could touch it. Using the sole of her foot, she pushed hard up against his belly, then slid her foot up and down. She felt his cock pulse, but not as wildly as it had done before. She curled her toes around his glans.

'Very hard, Master,' she said, looking him straight

in the eye. Leaving one hand on her breast, she moved the other down to her sex, watching his eyes follow it. Spreading her legs again and without taking her foot away from his phallus, she ran her fingers into her labia and found the entrance to her vagina. She pushed one finger inside, then withdrew it. She brought it up to her mouth and sucked it hard, tasting her own juices. Back at her sex, she pushed two fingers home this time and then three, letting Hadrian see how her labia were stretched apart, and just how much her vagina could accommodate. Again she brought her hand up to her mouth, this time sucking in all three fingers, her lips stretched around them just as the lips of her sex had been.

Suddenly, Hadrian lunged forward, scrambling on top of her prone body, so provoked by what he saw that he could control himself no longer. His mouth plunged down on to hers and she felt his tongue penetrate her lips, eager to glean a taste of her sex, too. His cock bumped against her belly.

Melinda quickly closed her legs, worried that his eagerness would allow him to get carried away again. She had planned to take it more slowly. But he was not in the mood to be refused. He pushed his strong muscled thigh between her legs. She struggled against him for a moment, but he was much too powerful for her; soon he had one leg inserted between hers. The second followed. She felt the underside of his cock pressing against her pubis.

'Yes,' he said. He slid further down her body and pushed his cock down between her legs and into her labia. The wetness there made it easy for him to find his target. Without hesitating, he rammed his cock up into her sex, feeling the hot silky flesh parting to admit him.

The heat, the wetness and the clinging flesh took him by surprise. His whole body shuddered with sheer pleasure. For a moment Melinda thought he was going to come. His hands gripped her body tightly and she felt his cock spasm inside her. He went rigid, every muscle locked. It was exactly what she'd feared would happen when he lunged at her. If he came a second time now, she *would* be sent away and he would never want to face her again. All the work she had done so far would be for nothing.

But he didn't. She felt his body begin to relax, the crisis passing slowly. He began to pump his cock into her, very deliberately at first, and then faster, his confidence in his ability to hold back evidently growing by the second.

'Yes . . .' he repeated, talking to himself.

He wrapped one arm around under her neck and kissed her hard on the mouth again, while his other hand squeezed between their bodies to feel for her breast. When he found it, he pinched her erect nipple.

'Master . . .' she gasped, the wave of sensation he produced taking her by surprise.

Hadrian's hips were rising and falling furiously, his strength and athleticism giving him stamina. His cock, as hard as a bone, was ploughing a furrow inside her.

Up until that moment Melinda had been playing a part. She had to bring him on, coax him back to erection, show him how quickly he could recover. She had aimed to make him feel like a man, not an inexperienced boy and she had succeeded. But her objective had had another unexpected effect. He was making her come. His long cock driving deep into her body, his tongue probing her mouth, his fingers playing at her breasts – all these things made her body

142

begin to heave with pleasure. The strokes of his cock were so powerful, the rest of his muscled body was pressing into her so hard, that he was irresistible. In seconds he had propelled her from calm calculation to throbbing need.

He felt her body change, too; felt the ripples of sensation coursing through her nerves. Knowing that what he was doing was having such an effect on her turned him on more. He had felt gauche and embarrassed, an inexperienced schoolboy in a world designed for men. But she had shown him how to overcome his inadequacies, and now he felt like a man, hard and strong and in control, both of himself and of her. He was able to make her feel, and to make her come.

Melinda felt his cock thrusting up into her, right to the neck of her womb. Her body tensed and she felt a tidal wave breaking over her so suddenly that it took her by surprise. She clung to his body as she came, gasping for breath, as every nerve in her body exploded with incandescent delight.

But though he felt it – especially in her sex which seemed as though it was trying to milk his cock, squeezing it rhythmically – he did not stop. The pistoning of his cock continued – wringing every last ounce of sensation from her orgasm – until she was feeble and weak.

He was in control. He felt his power. It was his turn now. He'd done what he wanted to do; he'd proved himself. Now Hadrian could allow himself to come. He slowed down his rhythm, and took his time. He let himself feel how Melinda's silky flesh parted as he penetrated her and hear her gentle gasps as he reached the height of his thrust.

'Oh, Master,' Melinda whispered, recovering her senses. 'Master, let me see you come . . .'

His stroke faltered. '*See* me?' He lifted himself up on his elbows so he could look down into her face, feeling proud that he could control himself so close to orgasm.

'Yes, Master. Come over my tits, so I can see your spunk.' She felt his cock throb its approval. In fact, he'd imagined doing such a thing, though never dreamt he'd find a woman so eager for him to do it.

He pulled out of her. His cock glistened, covered with her juices. He got to his knees at her side and grasped his cock.

'Like this?' he said.

'Oh yes, Master.'

But as he began moving his hand up and down on his cock, Melinda crawled down the bed. She was planning again. She wanted to make sure Hadrian had an experience with her that he'd never forget. Still on her back, she positioned herself between his legs, then pushed back until her face was between his thighs. As she saw him pumping his hand over his cock, she reached up with her tongue and probed his anus. She felt his body quiver as her tongue penetrated momentarily, then withdrew, making sure it had a good coating of saliva. As she moved her head back towards his cock, her hand felt for his buttocks and located the tight, wet hole.

'Master,' she said loudly, the sound vibrating against his balls, which were directly above her lips now. She extended her tongue and began licking them, teasing them to and fro, then lifting her head to suck them into her mouth. At exactly that moment, her finger plunged past his sphincter and into his rear passage.

The two sensations rushed through his body, excitements he had never felt before. His cock exploded in his hand, spunk jetting out of him in an arc so extended that most spurted down on Melinda's belly and thighs. Only the second wave – no less weak in the way it rocked his body, but not as pronounced in its trajectory – landed on her breasts.

He knelt there for a long time, milking the last drops from his cock, marvelling at how much there was despite the fact that he had already come only minutes before. Melinda's body was spattered with pearly white gobs of sticky fluid. Hadrian had never felt anything like it before, not physically or mentally. The idea of what she had done to him was just as exciting as the fact.

Eventually, he lifted himself off her, shuddering anew as she pulled her finger from his arse.

'Melinda,' he said, looking down at her. He could not stop himself grinning smugly.

'Oh, Master,' she said. 'It was wonderful.'

'You're wonderful. You really are. Can I see you again?' It was the sort of question he would pose in the real world. He still hadn't understood the rules of the society his father had created.

'Of course, Master.'

'Soon. I want it to be soon.'

'Master, you only have to ask.' She wasn't sure that was true, of course. The Emperor might not wish him to see one slave regularly. He might insist Hadrian was more catholic in his tastes.

'Oh Melinda, you've made me feel so good.'

'Thank you, Master.'

'Stop calling me Master.' He pulled aside the drapes of the bed and got to his feet as Melinda sat up. He looked seriously into her eyes. 'I don't want to be your Master. I want us to be friends. Do you understand? Will you be my friend?'

'Of course,' she said. It was odd not adding 'Master'.

The emotional impact of what had happened was written all over Hadrian's face. He looked like he couldn't quite take it all in at once. At the moment he was fixated on Melinda, unable to take his eyes off her. 'Is there anything I can do for you?'

'No,' she lied. 'Nothing.'

She hoped there was a great deal Hadrian could do for her, but now was not the right time to ask. She had accomplished her first objective more thoroughly than she had imagined was possible. And it was quite obvious from the way he was looking at her that Hadrian was besotted. If she played her cards carefully, he might prove to be her passport out of the villa.

'I'm going to speak to my father,' he said earnestly. 'He's going to have to release you. I'm not having you like this.'

'No!' she almost shouted. 'No, Hadrian. You mustn't.'

'I'm not going to leave you like this.'

'No, please . . .' If Hadrian told his father what had happened, the Emperor would immediately suspect the truth: that his son had become infatuated with the first slave he'd slept with and had no doubt been manipulated. 'This has to be our little secret . . . you must promise me.'

'Why?'

'Because . . .' She tried to find a convincing explanation that did not reveal the truth. 'Look, Hadrian, you're very young. You know what he will say. He'll say there are lots of girls to choose from, that you should have some of the others . . .'

'I don't want anyone but you, Melinda. I'm old enough to know what I want.'

'But he'll say you're not. It'll spoil all his plans for you, won't it?'

'Yes, but I really don't want all this, Melinda. I mean, it's not for me, really it isn't. But I know I want *you*.'

He was looking at her doggedly, his eyes full of what she could only describe as love. He had translated what she had done to him sexually into an emotional attachment.

'Oh, Hadrian,' she said. He pulled her to her feet and hugged her. 'There are so many things I want to do with you, so many things I want to show you.' She was manipulating him shamelessly, but she didn't care.

'Oh yes, I want to learn.'

'And I'll teach you. I have a feeling you're going to be a very good pupil.' She felt his penis throb slightly against her belly. 'But you've got to promise me that you will not tell your father. Not yet.'

'When then?'

'We'll work that out together. If you mention it now, he'll do something drastic, believe me. It's best to go along with him. Just do whatever he says. Ask to see me again, but not immediately or he'll suspect something. Then we can work it all out.'

'If you think that's best.'

'It is. Trust me.'

'Oh Melinda, you're so beautiful. I want us to be together.'

'Really?'

'Oh yes . . .'

There was no doubt that Hadrian had never meant anything more sincerely in his short life. It had worked out better than Melinda could have hoped. At the beginning of the evening she had seen a slim chance, a light at the end of a very dark tunnel. Now, it seemed that the light was getting brighter by the minute.

Seven

'All stand here,' Bandu commanded. The body slaves had been marched out into the courtyard by the four Nubians, and Bandu now indicated for them to stand along a wall in the full sunlight. As usual, they were all naked.

The nine women lined up as instructed, with their backs to the wall, facing the villa and the swimming pool. The sun had begun to sink but had not yet disappeared behind the roof of the main house. It was still hot.

They waited as the Nubians relaxed in the shade and guests came out of the villa to plunge into the pool.

Melinda had expected to be summoned by the Emperor all day. She feared, despite his assurances to the contrary, that Hadrian would not hold his peace and would go to his father, demanding that Melinda be released. If that happened, she knew her plan would fail.

Perhaps the body slaves being gathered in the courtyard was a prelude to a confrontation; it had never happened before.

As the sun beat down, and sweat beaded her naked body, Melinda's heart was in her mouth. The Nubians suddenly jumped to their feet; two male overseers were approaching from the villa, flanking a blonde woman. Her hair was long but scraped back and tied tightly in a chignon at the back of her head, which stretched the skin on her face, giving her a rather severe appearance. She was wearing a tight-fitting jerkin made from what appeared to be real snake skin. It revealed most of her shapely legs and was swollen by what was obviously a considerable bosom, though in every other respect the woman was slender. Her complexion was tanned, her skin a light-brown biscuit colour. In her left hand she carried a long bullwhip with a thick handle.

As she approached the line of body slaves, Melinda could see the cold piercing blue of her eyes. Her features were attractive but rather sharp and thin, with a small nose and delicate, lobeless ears. She had a long neck, the sinews of which were clearly defined.

She stopped in front of the first slave, eyeing her from head to toe. Using the coils of the whip, she lifted the body slave's breast, then pushed the whip between her legs. Melinda heard the girl gasp. 'Her,' she said at once. Though she spoke English, it was heavily accented with what Melinda thought might be Russian intonations.

The second slave in the row received the same treatment, but this time the woman passed her by. The third she merely looked at without touching. The fourth in the row was the petite blonde whom the Emperor had taken on the bed. The Russian, if that was what she was, lifted one of her heavy breasts with the whip and looked at the purple mark. 'Her,' she said to Bandu, who was following her down the line.

The fifth slave she touched with her right hand, running her finger over her mouth. The sixth she glanced at and said, 'Her,' without touching. It was Mollie. The seventh she touched with the whip, lifting both breasts and pushing the whip harshly between her legs but then passing on. The eighth in the line was Melinda. The cold blue eyes looked straight at her. The woman extended her right hand and wiped a bead of sweat from the top of Melinda's breast.

'Her,' she said, walking away, not glancing at the ninth slave in the line.

They were marched straight from the courtyard into the bathhouse. The four who had been chosen were held back while the others were bathed and taken to the dormitory. Bandu supervised them as the remaining five climbed into the tank and washed themselves. By the time they were dry, the Nubians had returned. Each oiled one of the four body slaves, as Bandu had done to Melinda before, and used the little pots of make-up.

By the time these preparations were complete, it was dark. Melinda had felt an enormous sense of relief that the line-up in the courtyard had nothing to do with her personal transgressions with Hadrian. Now she felt a sense of anticipation. Why the Russian woman had picked them she did not know, but Melinda had seen the way she'd looked at her and had found it thrilling.

The body slaves were arranged in single file and marched out of the bathhouse, through the courtyard – which was now totally deserted – and into the marble corridors of the house, the massive candles along the way all flickering with light.

Bandu led the way into the main hall, where everyone in the villa was already gathered around in front of the platform – the working slaves and overseers on one side, the guests on the other, and a gap left in the centre of the hall in front of the stone bench where Melinda had sat the first time she had been there.

The Nubians led the four selected slaves to the bench, then indicated for them to stand on it side by side. Their arrival was greeted with a great deal of comment, but the conversation ceased almost immediately as a brass fanfare echoed off the marble walls and one of the curtains on the arches was pulled aside.

The Emperor strode on to the rostrum. He was dressed like a Roman soldier, stiffened leather chest armour held in place by two shoulder-straps edged in gold, a tongued leather skirt, each strip also edged in gold, and calf-length sandal-like boots. The skirt and boots were both white. He carried the eagle-crested baton in his right hand while, with his left, he held the hand of the Russian woman, who was dressed just as she had been earlier that afternoon.

Mounting the steps to his throne, the Emperor sat down, draping one leg over its scrolled arm. He did not look happy. 'So,' he said. 'Make your final choice, Vacuna.'

Melinda remembered what Mollie had told her. The Russian woman was obviously a special guest, allowed her pick of the body slaves.

Vacuna came to the front of the rostrum and stared at the four naked women again. 'Her,' she said, pointing at Mollie. 'And her.' She had transferred her finger to Melinda.

'Are you sure?'

It might have been Melinda's imagination, but the Emperor seemed to become even less happy when Vacuna picked her.

'Yes.'

'Very well,' he said, grudgingly. 'Prepare.' He clapped his hands.

The Nubians had come up on to the rostrum. As

soon as the Emperor issued the order, they gathered around a large flagstone set immediately in front of the throne. Set into the stone were four metal flush-fitting handles. Each of the Nubians pulled up a handle and then used them to lift the stone up and to one side, grating it against the surrounding marble floor as they pulled it away. The assembled company moved closer to get a better view.

Underneath the stone was a pit about two feet square. As Melinda was led on to the rostrum by Bandu, she saw the pit was full of a dark, slightly purple-brown viscous substance resembling molten lava. It bubbled too, heated perhaps by an underground volcanic spring as many Roman houses had been.

'In,' Bandu said, pushing Mollie forward first.

Glancing sideways at Melinda, Mollie looked apprehensively at the purple mud. There were no steps down into the pit and she was not sure what she should do.

'In,' Bandu repeated, pushing her this time until both Mollie's feet were in the sludge.

For a moment, nothing seemed to happen. Then she began to sink. Her ankles disappeared and then her calves. Soon most of her thighs were under the surface. She stopped when the mud was halfway up her buttocks.

'You,' Bandu ordered.

Reluctantly, Melinda stepped on to the mud. Gradually she felt herself sinking, being sucked down into the volcanic slime. As it reached her sex it seemed to seep into her body, seeking out and invading every orifice.

Then Vacuna stripped off her snake-skin jerkin. She had a hard, muscular body and her breasts were supported by a primitive arrangement of leather straps, perhaps intended to be a Roman bra. As she pulled it away, Melinda saw that her breasts were heavy and pendulous, hanging down almost to her waist, their nipples pointing at the floor. She, too, lowered herself into the mud.

As Vacuna sank, Melinda felt her body pressing against her own. The pit was barely big enough for the three women.

When her feet touched the bottom, Vacuna grabbed Mollie around the waist and pulled her hard against her body. The effect was to trap mud between their navels, which then forced its way out like a volcanic eruption, up between their breasts and spattering their so far pristine upper bodies and faces. As the mud ran down her cheeks, the Russian kissed Mollie full on the mouth.

'Come on,' Vacuna said, glancing over her shoulder at Melinda. She reached out and pulled Melinda towards her until she was pressed against her side. Vacuna then moved around slightly so she became the filling in a sandwich formed by the two body slaves. She turned her head as far back as it would go and kissed Melinda on the side of the mouth. Apparently not satisfied with this, she turned round completely, so Mollie was at her back and Melinda in front. This time the kiss was full, her hand positioned on Melinda's neck to push their mouths together. At the same time, under the mud, Melinda felt a hand probing between her thighs.

The thought of lowering herself into the gooey, sticky mud had revolted Melinda. But now, much to her surprise, it was having a different effect. The purple sludge was warm and cohesive; it seemed to be rubbing against her body, holding her in a tight all-embracing grip. She was already sweating profusely and it was not only her body temperature that was rising; her sexual temperature had leapt, too. The mud was not harsh or abrasive but incredibly soft and sensual. It had the texture of oiled satin; it was also scented, giving off a musky aroma that made Melinda feel light-headed.

Vacuna's strong fingers found Melinda's clitoris and began to work against it. Melinda felt herself respond immediately. The mud invading her sex was so viscous that she found herself pushing down rhythmically against it.

Melinda looked at Mollie's mud-spattered face and could see the same reaction in her eyes, a mixture of puzzlement and excitement. Then she looked up. All around them, the guests and slaves were watching intently. Some of them had come up on to the rostrum to get a better view. She glanced up at the Emperor who looked, she thought, slightly less interested, though he *was* watching. He had an air of impatience about him, as though he wished it would all be over quickly.

Vacuna's other hand snaked over Melinda's buttocks. She felt Vacuna's finger searching for her anus, which it found, then pushed inside easily, as though the mud had already opened Melinda hydraulically.

Mollie moved to the side, creating waves in the mud that lapped against all three women's bodies. She positioned herself so the women formed a triangle, shoulder to shoulder, then leant forward to kiss Melinda on the mouth. In the secret hours they had spent together in the middle of the night there had been no contact, but Melinda felt a rush of tenderness as the Irish woman's tongue darted into her mouth and her hand cupped her muddy breast. She could see from the angle of her arm that Mollie's hand was heading for Vacuna's sex.

At that moment Melinda felt another penetration, fingers – one, then two – pushing into her sex. She felt herself swoon, the digits working up and down inside both the passages of her body, while the mud seemed to rub itself around and over and against her oily and pliant clitoris. The mud ran down her breasts, too, where it had been spattered, creating long fingers of sensation. Wanting more, she deliberately pushed herself down so the mud enveloped her right up to her neck. Vacuna followed, smiling, knowing exactly what Melinda was feeling.

Almost covered in the mud, Melinda felt her body tense as Vacuna's fingers stroked in and out. The viscous liquid felt like it was sucking everything – her breasts, her clitoris, the contours of her back, the muscles of her thighs – at the same time. As her body vibrated with pleasure, the mud also vibrated, fibrillating against her as though it were live tissue. She felt her body leap; then it released a wave of orgasm that spread up from her clitoris and out against the mud, shuddering against the ooze that held her so firmly.

'That's what I like,' Vacuna said quietly, withdrawing her fingers. She raised them out of the mud and beckoned to the Nubians. Bandu reached forward and handed her two large, white dildos, which looked as though they were made from bone, carved in detail to resemble a real cock, the acorn-like head of the glans and the thick tube of the urethra on the underside all accurately reproduced. But they had a flared base where the balls should have been, under which was a handle with a hand grip shaped to mould against the fingers.

Taking one in each hand, Vacuna plunged them into the purple-brown mud, causing a stir of delight among the watching crowd. All three women were now practically covered in mud, their hair, too, thoroughly caked with the oozing slime.

Vacuna was pushing one of the dildos between Mollie's thighs. She wanted it badly, having not only seen Melinda come so quickly, but felt the rippling mud transferring the shuddering sensation across the small gap between their bodies. As Melinda squeezed Mollie's large, melon-sized breasts with a muddy hand, Mollie opened her legs and maneouvred herself on to the fat head of the phallus. The inward pressure of the mud was so great, that she seemed compelled to move in slow motion.

The three women stood shoulder to shoulder again in a tight triangle, the mud seeming to transmit sensations from one to the other two. The mud was so sensual, so provoking; it was almost as if it were alive, moving against their bodies under its own impetus.

Melinda felt Mollie's body tremble as the dildo pushed into her sex. She brought her hand down to Mollie's buttocks and found the bud of her anus. It was as easy to penetrate as hers had been, the oily mud lubricating the passage. Inside, Melinda could feel the hardness of the dildo being thrust to and fro.

Vacuna used the tip of the second dildo on Mollie's clit, rubbing it hard and making her moan. Melinda brought her other hand up to Mollie's breast and pinched at her nipple. Just as Melinda had done, Mollie sank down to her neck, taking the other two with her, the mud engulfing her body.

'Oh sweet god in heaven . . .' she whispered, throwing her head back as her orgasm tore through her body. The shudders of passion rippled against the mud as it shuddered, too, seeming to magnify the overwhelming sensation.

As they straightened up, Vacuna smiled, her white teeth looking grotesque against her mud-covered face. She handed Melinda one of the dildos, and Mollie the other. 'Now me,' she said, in her Russian accent. Bringing her hand around the back of Melinda's neck, she pulled her into a kiss, plunging her tongue into Melinda's mouth and pushing their bodies together so suddenly that mud erupted between them.

As she broke the kiss, Melinda drove her hand down into the mud, holding the dildo like a sword. Her body still quivered from her orgasm which the mud seemed to hold within her, not allowing it to escape. She pushed the dildo up between Vacuna's legs and found the entrance to her sex.

'I want, I want...' Vacuna said, pushing herself down so hard on the head of the dildo she almost tore it from Melinda's hand. Fortunately, the density of the mud steadied it and Melinda regained her grasp as the phallus slid into Vacuna's body, right up to the flared base above the hand grip. Melinda felt the Russian wriggling her body against it, grinding her clitoris on the little ridge that had been purposefully carved at the bottom of the shaft.

Mollie closed in behind Vacuna. She too pressed the dildo down into the mud but this time from the rear. She wasn't sure what she was supposed to do, but she pressed the head of the dildo down between the Russian woman's buttocks. Surely she could not want it to penetrate there; it was too big. But as soon as Vacuna felt the head of the phallus nudging against her little ring of muscle she forced herself back down on to it, so powerfully that Mollie, too, almost lost her grip.

Melinda saw Vacuna looking around – her eyes wild – at all the faces watching her. She wanted them to know what was happening; being watched was part of her pleasure, too. Vacuna wriggled her body from side to side, rubbing her generous breasts against the surface of the mud, which seemed to suck at them, as though wanting to pull them down into its clutches.

Vacuna pulled Melinda forward so that their breasts were touching. Mollie closed in, too. Both body slaves had the same idea. Instead of holding the hand grip of the dildo, they slipped it between their thighs, squeezing it tightly. It was perfectly angled to be pushed up against their clitorises. Both instantly felt their orgasms revive, their nerves springing to life with new energy as the mud closed in on them. The three women clung to each other. They wrapped their arms around each other's backs, pressing tighter and tighter, wanting to share Vacuna's climax as they knew it would provoke their own.

Vacuna writhed and wriggled against them, the dildo in her rear too big for her. But the pain it caused translated to hot waves of pleasure in her sex, the dildo there pushing against the neck of her womb as she felt its hardness at her clit. She looked at all the faces staring down at her, all expectant, wanting to see more, the women wondering what it would be like, the men erect. Some of the men were already extracting their cocks from their robes and pushing them against the women.

Slowly, the Russian sank down, taking the other two women with her. The mud lapped at her breasts, holding them firmly, rubbing against them. Suddenly she felt a surge of pleasure, hard concentrated pleasure centred deep in her sex, like an arc of electricity flowing from the head of one dildo to the head of the other. She made a strange whining noise and her body shuddered uncontrollably, starting up new vibrations in the mud.

Melinda's body reacted instantly. She ground her clitoris against the handle of the dildo and felt the orgasm explode again. Its waves of sensation overwhelmed her, forcing her eyes closed. The mud, as it had done before, somehow trapped the feelings, amplifying them, like a storm in a canyon, unable to escape, rolling around and around until it was finally exhausted. In the darkness she felt Mollie come, too, the vibrations transmitted through the mud. Clinging together, the three women pressed themselves tighter, wanting to extract every last ounce of sensation from each other, the tiny ripples and aftershocks of orgasm causing new delights.

It was the feeling of being lifted that made Melinda open her eyes. The Nubians hauled her out of the mud bodily as the guests backed away. She watched as Mollie was also pulled out. Their bodies were showered with a spray of cold water; as the mud was washed away the appearance of each breast, buttock or belly was greeted with applause.

The shock of cold water was emotional as well as physical. As the pleasure of orgasm was swept away so cruelly, Melinda felt suddenly depressed. She looked up at the Emperor. He had clearly not enjoyed the spectacle and looked bored. He had called the other two body slaves up to the throne and was allowing them to extract his cock from the leather skirt he wore.

But that was not what depressed her most. As Vacuna pulled herself from the pit of mud to receive a round of applause, the Nubians led Mollie and Melinda off the platform, their bodies still dripping wet. For some reason Melinda glanced backwards –

perhaps for a last look at the Emperor – but behind him, lurking by the curtains pulled back on to the caryatid pillar of the arch, she saw Hadrian. His face was as white as a sheet and his expression clearly one of shock. If he saw her looking at him, he did not meet her eye.

Marched smartly through the house, Mollie and Melinda were returned to the dormitory. The leather helmets were pulled down over their heads, the gags forced into their mouths and the laces drawn tight. The manacles snapped around their wrists and the Nubians left without saying a word.

Melinda lay in the darkness, feeling more miserable than she had ever felt before at the villa. She could see the expression on Hadrian's face and knew exactly what it would mean. Alone with her, he had respected her, become infatuated with her, and had mistaken that infatuation for love because of what she had done for him. But he hadn't really appreciated what it meant for her to be a slave. He thought it was a game.

But now he knew. Now he had seen her used and abused, and willingly. He had seen she was a chattel, not a person. He'd seen Vacuna use her and how Melinda had enjoyed it. But worse, he'd seen how she was treated afterwards – washed down by the Nubians like an animal while the baying crowd applauded, then led away, no longer of any interest.

The whole situation must have been calculated to destroy his image of her, to shatter his dreams and cure his infatuation. His father wanted to show Hadrian her true slave-like nature. Hadrian would surely not want to see her again, and any chance of using him as a means of escape had been destroyed.

Melinda was glad of the blindfold. Behind it, she could shed a silent and invisible tear.

Eight

It had been four days since her experience with Vacuna; every hour of every day confirmed that she had been right about Hadrian's reaction to the spectacle. She had not seen or heard from him. He had not called for her as they had planned and she knew why.

Several of the other body slaves had been taken from the dormitory and Melinda suspected they were being used by Hadrian as well as his father. Having seen for himself what slaves would do, she was sure he had come to his senses and was indulging his appetites with catholic taste – applauded, no doubt, by the Emperor. He would never tell another slave, she was sure, that he did not wish to be called Master.

It was deeply depressing. The glimmer of hope – the light at the end of the tunnel – had faded, leaving her feeling more depressed than if there had been no hope at all.

But it was not only Hadrian's desertion that was affecting her mood. She was not being called to serve the Emperor like the other body slaves were. As thoughts of escape receded, the Emperor's neglect loomed large. Not only was she doomed to life at the villa, but she was going to have to accept that she no longer had a prominent place in the Emperor's affections. And, as with all the Masters she had known, the more she was denied their attentions, the more she yearned for them.

As usual, this evening the Nubians had come to hood and chain all the body slaves. It was a totally unnecessary action considering the electronic security, but a symbolic one, depriving the women of their ability to see and speak and move about. It reminded them that even these simple actions were controlled by the Master, that they were – and would remain – enthralled slaves. But so far the Nubians had not returned, as they had on the previous three nights, to take one or more of the slaves away.

The dormitory was quiet, except for the odd clink of a chain against the floor as one of the slaves moved in her sleep. Melinda prayed for sleep to come but her mind was too preoccupied with thoughts of the Emperor, and of Hadrian and what might have been. She tried to think why the Emperor had not called for her after looking at her so intensely and using her at the Festival of Juno. She could only imagine that he had been turned off by her activities in the mud pit. She had noticed that the display was not to his taste. Perhaps the fact that Vacuna had chosen her had somehow sullied Melinda in the Emperor's eyes. Perhaps he did not like his body slaves to respond so freely to the ministrations of a woman.

If that were the case, her future looked bleak. It would not be long before he found another slave to replace her, arranged another kidnapping or found a new recruit. She would then be relegated to the courtyard, to be worked during the day and used by the guests at night.

Eventually Melinda must have fallen asleep, because she woke with a start when the hand touched her. As her heart pumped wildly, driven by a rush of adrenalin, she realised it was probably only Mollie – who she hadn't spoken to since the mud pit – coming to talk after accomplishing her feat of escapology on the chain. She raised her head so the girl could unlace the helmet and, sure enough, felt fingers pulling the laces apart. As the helmet was pulled up over her head, it was not Mollie she saw in the dim light crouching in front of her, but Hadrian.

The sight made her heart pump even faster. He unsnapped the manacle at her wrist and held his finger to his lips, indicating the need for silence. Taking her by the hand, he led her quietly out of the dormitory and into the corridor.

'Here,' he whispered, pulling her into a small room used to store cleaning equipment. He closed the door behind them. Looking out of place among the Roman artefacts, he was dressed in trousers and a white shirt.

'How did you...?' Melinda was still stunned. There were so many questions whirling in her head, she could not think which to ask first.

'Oh, Melinda,' he said, hugging her to him. 'I'm so sorry.'

'Sorry?' Melinda pulled away, looking into his eyes.

'You told me not to do it, but I couldn't help myself. I just couldn't.'

'Do what?'

'Tell my father. I just couldn't help myself. After what I saw them doing to you. I couldn't let you go through that again, or anything like it. It was horrible. Horrible. I had to stop it.'

'You told him?'

'I told him what had happened between us. How

good it had been. I told him I wasn't prepared to see you treated like that again, that I wanted you to come away with me.'

'And?'

'He just laughed. He told me not to be so stupid, that you were just one of many, that I could have them all. That night he sent the Nubian to my room with another girl. This time she wouldn't leave. She was so strong . . .'

'What happened?'

'I don't want to think about it. I went to see him in the morning and told him my mind was made up, that I didn't want anyone else but you. So he said he was going to send me away, that I wasn't to ever come back here until I'd changed my attitude, that I was infatuated with you and was being stupid. You were right, you see. I shouldn't have told him. We should have planned it all in secret, then got away.'

'Did you go?'

'He flew me back to London. But I've got my own trust fund. I flew back to Rome on the next plane. I've hired a Jeep. There's a place we can go to in the north, outside Verona. He doesn't know anything about it. We'll be safe there. Will you come with me, Melinda? Will you? I haven't been able to think about anything else but getting you out of this awful place.'

'Oh, Hadrian.' Melinda felt a rush of emotion. The despair she had felt was instantly dispelled. The young boy staring at her so earnestly – his face wreathed in an expression of adoration – was her passport out of the villa and back to the OIM. Her plan had, after all, been successful. But her emotions were not confined to joy at the thought of freedom. She had a genuine affection for Hadrian; his happiness apparently rested on her decision. It wasn't fair, of course. She was using him. But what could she do? He *was* infatuated with her, just as he would have been with any of the other body slaves, had *they* been taken to his room that night. But his inexperience and gratitude at the way she had carefully overcome his initial sexual problem had transformed his infatuation into something far more serious.

'Will you, Melinda?' he repeated earnestly.

'Of course. You know it's what I want.'

He looked immensely relieved. If they did manage to escape, Melinda knew she must be very careful with him. She had no intention of going north with him, but she must make sure his feelings were not too badly hurt. After what he was going to do for her, she owed him that at least.

'I've got everything planned,' he said, bouncing up and down with excitement. 'After the games tomorrow . . .'

'What games?'

'There are to be Roman games in the afternoon, like in the Colosseum. Lots of guests. I've bribed one of the guards. It's all organised.'

'Look . . .' There was a small window in the store room, which overlooked the courtyard. Melinda had suddenly seen Bandu and one of the other Nubians marching across the paving-stones towards the dormitory, some sort of oil-lamp lighting their way. Hadrian followed her stare.

'What are they doing?'

'They're coming for one of us. I've got to get back.'

They both rushed out into the corridor and back into the dormitory. Running as fast as they could, Melinda threw herself on the straw palliasse and picked up the leather hood, pulling it down over her head as Hadrian struggled to get the manacle around her wrist. Footsteps echoed in the corridor outside, as Melinda closed her mouth around the big gag inside the hood. There was no time to lace it up. She heard Hadrian moving away. There were dark shadows at the far end of the room where she hoped he could hide and which, with luck, the light from the oil-lamps would not reach.

The dormitory door opened. Melinda tried to control her breathing and pretend she was asleep. Her heart was pounding so fiercely she thought they would be able to hear it. She didn't want to draw attention to herself.

'The door open,' she heard Bandu say. 'No bolt.'

'They not going anywhere,' the other Nubian said. 'Should be bolted.'

The footsteps crossed the room. As they approached, Melinda realised they were coming for her. They were bound to notice the laces were undone and would certainly raise the alarm, especially after finding the door open. They would search and find Hadrian; this time his father would make sure he never got back in again.

Bandu knelt by Melinda's side and unsnapped the manacle at her wrist. Melinda pretended to start awake. They pulled her into a sitting position and turned her head to unlace the hood.

'You do this?' she asked, showing the other Nubian the loose lacing.

'No, I lace tight.'

Bandu pulled the hood from Melinda's head. 'Check others,' she ordered.

Melinda watched as the black woman took the oil-lamp and bent over each body slave in turn, waking them and turning them over to check the lacing on the hood. As she got to the far end, the light from the lamp spilled into the shadows. Melinda could see Hadrian's modern shoes. She held her breath.

'They tight, all tight,' the woman said, coming back. The shadow returned to cover Hadrian again.

'Someone sloppy.'

Bandu pulled Melinda to her feet, thankfully not making a connection between the open door and the untied laces.

Melinda's heart calmed slightly as they marched out of the dormitory and into the main house. But she was still worried. It was very late and as far as she knew none of the body slaves had ever been called to the Emperor at this time of night. She hoped the unexpected summons and Hadrian's appearance were mere coincidences, that her presence was not required because Tiberius had discovered his son's plans and wanted to chastise Melinda as a result.

Just as hope had risen again it seemed as though it were to be snatched away for a second time. As they mounted the stairs, Melinda became more and more convinced that the only reason she was being taken to the Master at this hour was to be interrogated about Hadrian and told that his plan had been foiled.

Bandu swung one of the big carved doors open and led Melinda inside. They did not walk through the curtain that divided the room but turned to the left where the silk drapes that hung on all the other walls had been drawn aside to reveal plain white stone. Set into this were four metal rings: two at well over head height and spaced six feet apart, and two immediately below them just above the floor. White ropes were tied to each ring. To one side was a small table on which were placed a large bowl of water and a small brush made from an assortment of twigs bound together by a thong of leather.

The two Nubians placed Melinda facing against the wall. They wound the ropes around her wrists, tying them so her arms were stretched out and up on either side of her body. The women dropped to their knees and quickly spread her legs, tying her ankles with the rope attached to the lower rings. The white rope bit into her soft flesh. Her body formed a large X against the white wall, her breasts pressed against the stone, which was far from smooth and scratched her skin.

The Nubians left. She heard the heavy door being closed. The room was silent. Melinda's feelings were confused. She felt her body coursing with the familiar excitement bondage always created in her, an excitement that centred on the little nut of her clit. It throbbed like a little pump, waves of sensation flooding out from it. But it could not overcome her other emotions. She was still afraid that the reason for the Emperor's summons, and for her bondage, had nothing to do with his sexual desire for her, but was entirely due to the activities of his son.

If Hadrian had never appeared she would have found this experience unequivocally exciting – the Master calling for her alone, and having her prepared in this way. It was, after all, what she had yearned for. Now, with the prospect of escape revived again, her feelings were totally confused.

'Are you waiting for me?' The high-pitched voice came from the other side of the dividing curtain, but Melinda had not heard any footsteps or noise to indicate the Emperor's entry. Had he been sitting there all the time? She heard the silk rustle as he parted it. 'You look very uncomfortable. Are you?'

'Yes, Master.'

'Do the ropes hurt?'

'Yes, Master.'

'I bet they do. You find it exciting, don't you?' The Emperor came up behind her. From the corner of her eye she could now see him. He was naked, but for an arrangement of straps around his hips which supported a harness wrapped around his fully erect cock. The harness was composed of three thin belts, one under his balls and around the bottom of his shaft, the other two forming a V-shape between his balls, separating them and holding them up and out. The belts were tight and made the blood vessels and veins on his cock stand out prominently. The leather around his hips was studded with jewels, diamonds and emeralds, spaced along its length.

He extended his hand to caress Melinda's pert, round arse. He was carrying a short leather whip in his other hand. 'You have to be punished, don't you?'

'Yes, Master.' Her worst fears were instantly confirmed. She was here to be punished because the Emperor knew of his son's plans.

His hand travelled down between the cleft of her buttocks until he was touching her shaven labia. She knew he could feel how wet they were, but he made no comment.

'You have to be punished,' he repeated, 'for what you have done. This pretty little arse has got to be whipped. You're very lucky I'm going to deal with you personally, aren't you?'

'Oh yes, Master.' That was perfectly true.

'I know what you did. Filling his head with all sorts of ideas, taking advantage of him. Didn't you?'

'No, Master.'

'Don't argue with me. Didn't you?'

'Yes, Master.'

'Yes. Yes, you did. Fortunately he is young. He

will soon get over you. He'll soon realise what all this can mean to him, that he can have everything he desires . . .'

Melinda cringed inwardly. He knew it all.

'I can't imagine what you thought you were doing. Perhaps you didn't think. Did you?'

'No, Master.'

She felt him rubbing the tip of the whip along her naked back.

'So I've sent him away. Back to London. When he comes back, maybe next year, I know he'll see things differently. He'll be ready to treat slaves as they should be treated.'

Melinda could not believe what she was hearing. He was telling her Hadrian had been sent away and would get over her. He clearly knew nothing about what had happened since he'd sent his son away. He didn't know Hadrian was back, which meant he didn't know what he was planning.

'As for you, I decided to let you stew in your own juices for a while, so you could contemplate what it would be like without your Master. Was that how you repaid me, after all my kindness to you?'

Melinda's relief was so total she forgot to reply.

'Was it?' the Emperor barked.

'No. No, Master.'

'But I must have my fun too, mustn't I?'

'Yes, Master.'

'I will teach you a lesson, which I do not expect you to forget. Is that understood?'

'Yes, Master.'

'Punishment. It excites you, doesn't it?'

'You know it does, Master.'

He had seen the excitement in her face, sensed perhaps the surge of hope she had felt as she realised all was not lost. But what she'd said was not a lie. Her buttocks felt sensitive and vulnerable. She could still feel the impression of the whip on them. It was a long time since she had been whipped.

'I'm giving you one more chance.'

She wriggled slightly, involuntarily, dismissing thoughts of Hadrian for the moment. Her body asserted its own needs, the heat created by the bondage was demanding her full attention. The Master was cross with her but he still wanted her, perhaps even needed her. He had ignored her as a means of punishment but, she suspected, it was his own needs that had made him bring her to him tonight. Punishing her personally was not as effective as having the Nubians whip her on the stone in the courtyard in front of the guests, but it was more exciting for him. He wanted her. He had obviously been thinking about her. In other circumstances, such thoughts would have made her swoon with pleasure.

His hand ran over the curves of her buttocks again. She could feel the heat of his cock radiating against her thigh. He slapped her left buttock lightly with the palm of his hand, then moved away. 'Did you know that about fifty years ago Julius Caesar discovered a very interesting fact?' The fifty years he referred to were, in fact, more like two thousand.

'No, Master.'

He picked up the little twig brush and dipped it in the bowl of water. 'He discovered, quite by accident, I understand, that . . .' He flicked the water over Melinda's bottom, dipped the twig again and showered her for a second time. '. . . water has an amplifying effect on the strokes of a whip.' He raised the short whip and slashed it down on Melinda's moist behind. 'From that day on, all his slaves, of which he had many, naturally...' He raised his arm and delivered a second stroke. '... were punished in this way.' A third stroke followed. 'Apparently it was very effective.'

The pain seared through Melinda's body. It was true; the water seemed to make the whip vibrate more, sting more. She felt three red-hot weals burning across her buttocks, the pain travelled down to her sex, where it was twisted into a sensation of almost unbelievable pleasure. She wriggled against her bonds, their constraint adding to her excitement.

The Emperor dipped the twigs again. 'Is it true?'

'Yes, Master. Oh, yes.'

'Good, good. Keep still.'

He flicked the water over her bottom again. Momentarily it cooled the heat of the weals. 'He was a clever man, a very clever man.' He slashed the whip down diagonally, so it crossed the three existing weals. 'An Empire-builder, of course...' The fifth stroke was diagonal, too. '...but then I shall build my Empire. And you will be one of its slaves. The OIM has had its day. I shall build a new, bigger and better organisation and you will have the privilege to serve it.' He raised the whip higher still and slashed it down. The thwack of leather on flesh reverberated throughout the room.

The last blow made Melinda gasp, but not from pain. The throbbing sexual heat that coursed through her body instantly turned the surge of pain to another jolt of pleasure and took her breath away. Each stroke had charged her nerves, had accumulated like the charge in a battery. The last stroke had released it all, making sparks of excitement fly out in all directions.

'Little bitch...' the Emperor mumbled. He could

see Melinda's condition, the way her body was squirming with pleasure. He touched her buttocks, stroking the six red weals he had produced. Melinda moaned. It was as if he were touching her clitoris, so sensitive did they feel, each converting instantly into a new erogenous zone.

'Master...' she whispered, though she knew she shouldn't.

Better still, he came up behind her and pressed himself against her back, dropping the whip, pushing his hands between the walls and her breasts so he could cup them against his palms and feel her stone-hard nipples as he pushed his harnessed cock into the deep cleft of her arse. She felt its heat against the warmth the red weals were generating. She felt it throb. She wanted his cock so badly she tried to push her bottom back against him, so it would slip down between her legs.

'I know what you want, you little bitch,' he said.

'Yes, Master. Please, Master.'

'Tell me then. Let me hear it.'

'Please, Master. Use me, Master. Put your cock in me, Master.'

He rubbed the palms of both his hands against her nipples, pressing them back on to her chest, then bucked his hips so that his cock pushed down between her legs and into her thick puffy labia. He slid it back and forth, enjoying the heat and wetness he had created.

'Shall I heat you up again?' he whispered in her ear, letting his hot breath blow into its inner folds.

'No, Master...' Melinda was too desperate to know what she was saying. Her whole body ached for the release of penetration. 'Yes, Master,' she corrected. 'Anything you want, Master.'

The tip of his cock nudged into her clitoris. It was like an electric shock; her body shuddered, she gasped. But he slid his cock back a little, wanting to tease her. He could feel the need he fuelled, the heat radiating from her bottom, the tension in her every nerve. He held his cock there between her labia, wanting her to feel it, pushing it up against her but not into her. For her, it was so near and yet so far from what she really wanted.

In her mind's eye she could see his cock, veined and swollen by the straps, her labia closed around it like a mouth, sucking on it, her juices flowing over it and making it glisten.

'Is this what you want?' he whispered, pushing his cock harder against her.

Suddenly he plunged it into her, into a flood of juices in her sex that felt like a warm torrent. Holding on to her tightly by her breasts, hugging her back on to him, he angled his cock up into her – once, twice, then for a third time – each stroke higher and deeper.

Melinda couldn't believe it. She had got what she yearned for. Her Master had used her body, had allowed her to come over his cock. She hardly had time to think about it before the nerves in her body knitted together as one, a tight ball of sensation that, as she pulled deliberately on the ropes that held her, exploded into orgasm. She felt everything all at once, every stimulus and provocation – the weals on her arse, the bite of the ropes, the hands on her nipples and the hard cock buried inside her.

'Oh, Master,' she cried loudly, as her body shook under the impact of the assault on her nerves. It was a long time before her body was still.

Slowly, with unexpected tenderness, he pulled out of her. He could have called the Nubians to untie her, but he did it himself. She sank to the floor, her thigh muscles so stretched they could not support her weight.

The Emperor parted the drapes that divided the room and went to sit on the bed, his cock and the leather wrapped around it soaked with her juices.

'Here,' he said imperiously.

Melinda got to her feet, supporting herself against the wall, then walked through the curtain a little unsteadily. She had come so copiously her juices were trickling down both her thighs. On the other side of the curtain she saw that a small table had been drawn up by the foot of the bed. On it was a leather harness not dissimilar to the one around the Emperor's waist. Next to it was another arrangement of straps very like a horse's bridle, but with a bit made from what looked like bone. There was also a small glass pot containing a thick, white cream.

'Put that on,' the Emperor said, indicating the harness.

Melinda picked it up. She saw she could step into it like a pair of panties; she also saw that it held a wide but not very long dildo, its flared base secured into a leather pad attached to the front of the harness. She hesitated for a second, there could only be one use for the dildo.

'Do it,' the Emperor snapped.

Melinda slid the leather up over her hips. Two buckles on either side could be adjusted to hold it tightly in place. The dildo poked out from her loins as though she had grown a cock.

The Emperor picked up the bridle-like leather and took the white bone of the bit between his teeth. Two metal rings held it on either side of the mouth and were attached to a leather strap which he secured around his head, buckling it tightly. The bit in place, the Emperor knelt up on the bed on all fours. There was little doubt what he wanted. 'You know what to do,' he said, the words slightly muffled by the bit. It was clearly not intended as a gag.

Melinda's reluctance at the idea made her hesitate again.

'Don't make me cross,' he warned.

She got up on to the bed, then reached for the pot of cream. She smeared it on to the head of the dildo, and then took another big dollop which she applied to the cleft of the Emperor's upturned buttocks. Putting the pot down again, she nudged the head of the dildo forwards into his arse. She found that, by moving her hips, she could force it back and forth. As there was no feeling from it, she had to guide it with her hand.

'Yes,' he grunted, as she found the right place. He clenched his teeth on the white bit and pushed himself back against her to achieve the first penetration. Pain seared through him. 'Hhh . . .' he gasped, wanting her to push, too. She bucked her hips, like a man would do. The dildo slid home right up to the leather that held it. She wondered if the boyish Plania had been used in this way.

'Hhh . . .' he mumbled again, moving his buttocks to indicate she should move the dildo in and out.

Melinda had experienced many strange things with the Masters, but nothing like this. She bucked her hips to and fro just as if she were a man. The base of the dildo ground against her clitoris on the inward push and a wave of hot pleasure flooded over her. Her body was oversensitized by the power of her orgasm, the lightest touch provoking a massive surge of feeling. Her mind told her she didn't want to be doing this, but the messages from her body were entirely different.

'Now ... I show you ... the Roman way ...' the Emperor said haltingly, the pain he relished making it difficult for him to speak. He reached behind his back and caught her by the hand, pulling it round in front of him and wrapping her fingers around his cock, still wet from her juices.

As she pushed forward, he pushed his cock between the ring of her fingers. The pain from the dildo tore into his every nerve. His jaws clenched on the white bone between his teeth. She was moving faster, the dildo slick with cream. Her hand began working on his cock, rubbing up and down on the rim of the glans. The harder she rubbed, the more the pain seemed to turn to a sharp, burning, needling torment; still pain, but so close to sexual pleasure and so stimulating that he could not tell the difference.

He felt his spunk pumping into his cock. He was ready. With an enormous effort, he twisted his head up and back to look at her, to watch as she used her newly acquired cock on him, just as if she were a man, except her breasts were riding up and down on her chest with each movement. He looked at her face and saw her distaste, but he could also see her desire.

He dropped his head back, looking down his body to his cock. He watched the way her delicate, slender fingers circled it so expertly, milking the spunk out of him. He managed to watch as the ring of her fingers rubbed over the rim of his glans one final time; his cock jerked in reaction, shooting a stream of white spunk out from the narrow slit of his urethra and down over the silk sheets. Then his eyes rolled back and he could only feel as the rest of his seed shot out in a long arc, his whole body shuddering. Even after the volcanic eruption, spunk continued to ooze out of him as her hand squeezed and pulled and kneaded to make sure – as she had been trained to do – that every last drop was wrung out of him.

Nine

They were left in the dormitory – chained to the straw palliasses in the tight leather hoods – much longer than they had ever been before. It was not until mid-morning that the Nubians came to collect the body slaves from their quarters and take them to the bath-house. As they were allowed to bath they could see, out in the courtyard, a bustle of activity. The working slaves were busy in the outbuildings polishing and cleaning equipment, while the horses were all being groomed, and their saddlery and tack rubbed with saddle soap.

Tables had been placed around the pool; more guests than Melinda had ever seen before at the house were having what appeared to be a late breakfast between dips in the pool.

After their ablutions, the body slaves were not taken back to the dormitory. Instead they were marched out into the courtyard, where, while the guests admired their naked bodies – pointing out to each other who they thought had the nicest hair, or legs, or breasts – Bandu produced a long, heavy chain. Attached to the chain at regular intervals were nine manacles. With the help of the other Nubians, she saw to it that the left wrist of each of the body slaves was manacled to the chain. As soon as this task was completed, she took the top end of the chain and began leading the slaves across the courtyard and out into the clearing beyond the back of the house.

The sun was hot but they soon reached the forest of trees that surrounded the villa on all sides, and the shade they provided was welcome. A path had been worn by frequent use through the lush undergrowth. The slaves were compelled to walk in single file; the three other Nubians followed behind.

As she walked, Melinda tried to collect her feelings. Her night alone with the Emperor after so much neglect, had left her body humming, like the string of a musical instrument resonating long after the last note had been played. He had allowed her a privilege few Masters would grant and, though she knew it was not right – that he was not really a Master – it thrilled her profoundly.

That did not mean she was any less set on escape. She had half-expected Hadrian to visit her again after Bandu had returned her to the dormitory. She had lain awake waiting, but the hood had remained tightly laced and eventually she had fallen asleep. As their meeting had been so rudely interrupted, she had no idea what he planned to do. All she remembered him saying was that it would be 'after the games'.

All the extra activity in the villa presumably related to the Roman games he had mentioned, but Melinda had no idea what they were or what the body slaves would be required to do. She could only wait and see.

The trees began to thin out. Soon the procession of women was walking into a large clearing; at the end of it was an incredibly steep cliff, jutting out from the ground at almost ninety degrees.

Bandu led the party straight over to it. As they approached, Melinda saw a dome-shaped entrance to what was obviously a cave partially obstructed by overhanging plants. From closer still she could see what was clearly the work of mankind; the entrance had been enlarged, and there were stone chisel marks like fish scales on the walls.

The slaves were marched inside. The evidence of ancient endeavour was all around them, long steps carved into the floor of the tunnel, chisel marks all over the rounded walls. The tunnel curved to the right, cutting off the light from the entrance, and Melinda became aware of a source of artificial light, a long tube that ran overhead.

The tunnel got increasingly deeper and broader, and though the stone-carving marks were still evident, it was obvious the widening was mostly a natural phenomenon. This was certainly the case when the tunnel emerged into a large underground cavern in the shape of two saucers, one reversed on top of the other – an almost perfect elliptical shape. The stone floor had been hewn down to form step-like seats, like an amphitheatre, with the centre flattened into what was obviously intended to be the arena. Above, in the concave roof, modern electrical spotlights lit the whole space. A flight of shallow steps led down to the centre, and then up again to a gallery on the other side, neatly bisecting the whole basin. In a central position in the seating, a box had been constructed which contained a throne not unlike the one on the platform in the grand hall of the villa.

Bandu led them down to the floor of the arena, then up the other side. At the top of the steps a very narrow corridor had been carved entirely by hand. On each side of the corridor were heavy wooden doors with metal bars, through which small individual cells could be seen. As they walked past, Melinda glimpsed men and women inside the cells, their bodies mostly dressed like Roman gladiators. At the end of the passage was a bigger door, through which they were led. The room beyond had been carved from solid rock. The body slaves were pushed inside. The Nubians did not follow.

Stacked against the wall in their new accommodation were five black metal triangles identical in design to the triangle Melinda had been suspended from, except that the leather harnesses which had been secured around her body were already clipped into the metal rings on the frame.

It was cool in the cave; the body slaves sat on the rock floor, hugging themselves for warmth. Melinda sat next to Mollie, who smiled at her sympathetically, a look of puzzlement on both their faces. Melinda wanted to tell Mollie everything that had happened to her last night but did not dare speak. Not only was the rule of silence deeply engrained in her but she knew the Emperor's devotion to Roman authenticity did not exclude modern conveniences like electric light. He was just as capable of using microphones and transmitters to check what they were saying. She certainly did not want to risk jeopardising any plan Hadrian might have.

No one else dared to speak, so they waited in silence. It was at least an hour before they heard noises – distant but distinct, the tramp of feet on the stone – which they took to be people taking their places in the arena outside.

'You.' Bandu had entered and was pointing at Sulpicia. 'And you,' she pointed at the redhead. 'And you.' This time the finger pointed at Melinda. She selected five girls in all.

As the other three Nubians began lying the metal

triangles on the floor, Bandu took Sulpicia by the arm and led her over to the first frame.

'Lie down, face down,' she ordered, when the slave was standing inside the triangle with her feet at its base. As soon as she obeyed, the Nubians all helped to buckle the straps around Sulpicia's ankles, knees, thighs, waist and upper chest. Her hands were drawn up over her head and secured into the cuffs at the triangle's apex.

Each of the other four girls were made to lie in a black metal triangle, and then strapped into it. The four other body slaves watched, wondering whether they should be disappointed or relieved at having been left out.

Melinda wriggled uncomfortably. The metal frame was heavy and pushed her naked body against the rough stone floor. In this position, her upper arms forced her head down and cramped her shoulders.

From the arena they heard a fanfare and then a burst of applause. Melinda imagined the Emperor making his entrance down the shallow steps and taking his seat on the throne.

'Let the games commence.' His voice echoed around the cavern, reaching the body slaves quite distinctly.

There was another round of applause, followed after a few minutes by the 'oohs' and 'aahs' of some kind of sporting event. This went on for some time before what was clearly a round of applause for a winner.

The door of the cell opened and five men entered, all dressed in the leather body armour of Roman gladiators – straps across their chest – and short leather skirts. Their muscular bodies had been oiled and glistened, and each carried three wheels, obviously made from modern materials, that were the size of bicycle wheels. Each man also carried what looked like a small saddle.

By twisting her head to one side Melinda could see the man who approached Sulpicia. He hoisted the corner of the triangle by her left foot into the air and screwed the hub of the wheel into a shank fitted on the angle of the frame. The second wheel was fitted on the other side in the same way, and both were tightened with a very un-Roman spanner. The third wheel was fitted into a fork-shaped housing. The base of this was bolted into a shank on the apex of the triangle, which allowed the wheel to be moved for steering by pulling on two reins attached to either side. With all three wheels fitted, Sulpicia's body was about a foot off the ground.

The man now fitted the saddle. Two light metal bars were screwed into the frame of the triangle in the middle; the saddle was fitted across them right behind Sulpicia's fleshy and naked buttocks.

Melinda felt her frame being lifted; soon the wheels had been bolted in place. Once the saddle was fitted, she felt her rider trying it for size and making some small adjustments.

Judging by the noise outside, another event was in progress. A round of applause indicated it was over.

The five women were strapped helplessly into their metal frames, their bodies unable to move, breasts hanging down towards the floor, buttocks sticking up. Five human chariots. The riders stood expectantly at the apex of each, waiting for the signal. Melinda caught Mollie's eye. From the expression on her face, she could tell Mollie was glad she was not tied into one of the contraptions.

Outside there was another brass fanfare. The riders

pulled the chariots forward by the reins attached to the front wheel. They trundled them down the narrow corridor – only just wide enough to take them – and out into the main cavern, the wheels jarring on each step as they were pulled down to the floor of the arena.

'Ladies, gentlemen, Romans. You have seen the wrestling and the jumping. Now, I present for your entertainment, the chariot race.' The Emperor's voice was followed by a rapturous round of applause.

Melinda twisted her head but could see very little. Her view was restricted to the first row of stone seats and the floor of the arena itself, which was covered in sawdust. She could see the chariots being lined up by the Nubians, who then handed each rider a long wooden pole. The riders swung themselves into the saddle, putting their feet up on either side of the metal frame, their legs bent at the knee, taking the reins in one hand and the pole in the other.

'Ready . . .' the high-pitched voice of the Emperor shouted. 'Go . . .'

Melinda felt herself lunge forward, the rider using the pole like the oar of a punt, driving it against the ground on one side of the frame with his right hand, steering with his left. The speed of the chariot was surprising, or perhaps just seemed to be, as Melinda's face was so close to the ground. Soon the chariots gained momentum and began jostling for position, their rear wheels clashing and grinding together as one rider tried to push another to one side.

The sawdust kicked up into Melinda's eyes. She tried to close them but that made her feel giddy, so she narrowed them as much as she could. The movement of the chariot strained the leather straps, her body weight thrown one way and then another, as they cornered the circular track.

Melinda was not in front. She could only gain fleeting impressions, but thought she and her rider were second or third. But their speed increased and she saw them steering past another chariot as the crowd cheered and bayed on their favourite.

Round and round they went, the naked bodies of the slaves, strapped into the frames, quivering and trembling and covered with dust. Looked at one way, it was the ultimate humiliation, the slaves used as mere components of a machine. But from another angle it was an expression of what they were – not individuals with feelings and desires – but objects to be used in whatever way their Master wanted them used. The more extreme the use, the more Melinda felt – and all the others like her – that she was reduced to what she craved most, her will stripped away, her submission total. Despite the dirt and discomfort, Melinda could feel her body churning with excitement.

But her sense of exhilaration was matched by her rider's. As he drove forward she felt his cock nudging into her buttocks, the sight of her naked body, the shaven labia between her open thighs, provoking him as it was intended to do. The saddle was positioned perfectly. As his cock grew, it pushed between her buttocks. It only needed to be slightly adjusted for it to be angled down into her labia.

The crowd roared their approval as they saw what was happening. All the riders had erections. All had manoeuvred their cocks towards the body slaves' sexes. While still concentrating on driving the chariots forwards, they were all trying to push their cocks into the women. All found their labia wet, the slaves' excitement heightened by their position.

As soon as she felt the rider's erection, Melinda

knew this was not an accident but part of the race. The Emperor's imagination had been at work. It was not only who could go faster but who could take the slave at the same time. She wriggled against the cock of her rider and felt it slip into the opening of her sex. Suddenly it was inside her; not deep, but there, wallowing in her wetness. She heard the crowd applaud simultaneously – whether for this feat or some other she did not know.

Her rider drove forward, trying to keep the chariot speeding around the track at the same time as he tried to push his phallus into her. He shifted in the saddle, moving right on to the edge so he could achieve maximum penetration. Melinda pushed back too, feeling him slide deeper – wanting him there, wanting to win, craving the Emperor's approval – everything else forgotten. Races usually had prizes. She wanted to win the prize. Perhaps it was another night like last night, a night alone with her Master. That would be the best prize of all.

Then she thought of Hadrian and her escape. What if they *did* win? It might change everything. There was no telling what would happen or where they would be taken. Surely it would be better if they lost; she would be taken back with all the other slaves and Hadrian must be counting on that. If only he'd had a chance to tell her his plans.

Despite her excitement, Melinda tried to pull her buttocks forward and away from her rider's erection. It slid outwards and, as they bumped around a corner, came out altogether. He managed to push it back in again but could not manage to hold it there. It bounced up and down against her labia. Melinda heard jeers from the crowd.

As they turned, Melinda saw a chariot overtake

them, the rider's efforts to reposition his cock reducing their forward speed. Just at that moment there was a cry of delight from the crowd and a round of applause. Almost immediately Melinda felt their speed decrease. The race was over; one of the others had won.

All the chariots drifted to a standstill.

'*Pute*,' her rider hissed, taking one of the reins and slapping it hard across her buttocks as he dismounted.

The four Nubians ran into the arena and began unstrapping the four losing slaves from the frames. As Melinda's legs were released, she fell to her knees, the pain and soreness from the straps much greater now she was free. When her hands were released, she tentatively eased them back against her cramped shoulders and felt another bite of pain. She looked across the arena. It was obvious that Sulpicia had won. Her rider stood proudly with a garland of laurels on his head, Sulpicia's buttocks spattered with his seed. The race had obviously depended on the first ejaculation as well as the position of the chariot.

Looking up, Melinda saw that everyone from the villa had been brought to the arena, and was sitting or lying on the stone steps, supplemented with cushions. The overseers sat by the working slaves while the guests were massed together, all wearing antique Roman garb. Many of the guests had been excited by the proceedings and were engaging in some sort of sexual activity, with each other or with a working slave they had extracted from the pack. A small white-haired man was sitting with one of the slaves kneeling between his legs, his erection buried in her mouth, while another slave sat behind him rubbing her breasts against his back. Two women guests had a male guest seated between them and were both fingering his body idly, his cock sticking out from the folds of his toga. Another man had taken a female guest on to his lap. From the position of her robe and the expression on her face it was obvious that his cock was impaled inside her.

The Emperor was in his special box, sitting on the throne accompanied by the four body slaves – including Mollie and Plania – who had not been chosen for the race. He was wearing a short white tunic from which Plania, who sat on his knee, had extracted his cock; she was playing with it aggressively. Mollie was kneeling at his feet and caressing his leg, while the other two slaves stood on either side of him, their naked bodies within easy reach.

Melinda had been right. Sulpicia and her rider were left in the ring, while the four Nubians led each of the losers up the steps and into the funnel-shaped corridor that led outside. Melinda was glad she had not won the prize.

As they walked through the stone tunnel, Melinda's heart was in her mouth, expecting Hadrian's plan, whatever it was, to spring into action at any minute. But it did not. They walked out into the sun, its brightness making their eyes water after the artificial light in the cavern. They were soon relieved by the shadows of the trees.

They walked in single file again, this time with a Nubian between each slave, but without the manacles – they obviously felt it was unnecessary now they were one-to-one. If Hadrian planned to snatch her now, Melinda feared for the result. The Nubians were strong and he would not stand a chance against four of them.

But he did not. They reached the clearing round

the villa and marched into the courtyard which, like the villa itself, was deserted. Bandu led them into the bathhouse and ordered them to bath. Their bodies were filthy, the dust and dirt from the arena stuck to their bodies with their sweat.

The water in the tank was warm and the four slaves bathed together, helping each other to wash away the grime with soap and big natural sponges. They washed their hair and scrubbed out their ears and all their other bodily crevices. Finally clean, they climbed out and were given towels to dry themselves.

Melinda's heart would not stop pounding. After all, it was now 'after the games'. She looked around continually, expecting to see Hadrian appear at any minute, though hoping, at least while the Nubians were around, that he wouldn't. If he waited until they were returned to the dormitory, however, it would be an excellent time. The villa would still be deserted.

The trouble was they were not taken to the dormitory – or at least Melinda wasn't. As soon as she was dry, Bandu picked up a leather collar, strapped it around Melinda's neck and clipped a gold chain into it at the front under her chin. Without a word, or a flicker of an expression, she led Melinda out into the courtyard, leaving the others behind.

They walked into the main house, along the echoing marble corridors and up the stairs, but at the top of the staircase took a different direction along a corridor that led away from the Emperor's bedroom. It seemed as if they had walked the whole length of the villa when they arrived at a door, which Bandu opened.

'In,' she said, dropping the chain.

Melinda walked into the room. It was a small bedroom – a wooden-framed double bed, a wooden chest to one side of it, and a chair the only furniture. There was a small window, over which a thick beige curtain, filtering the afternoon light, had already been drawn.

'On the bed,' Bandu said, as she removed the collar from Melinda's neck.

For a moment Melinda was puzzled. Why had she been brought here? All the guests were still at the games. Had the Emperor granted a special request and allowed one of them to indulge his preference for Melinda? And if that were the case, how would it interfere with Hadrian's plans?

It was only when Bandu reached behind her back, undid the fastenings of the leather halter and slipped it off her shoulders, that the truth dawned. It was Bandu who intended to take advantage of the empty house.

She shucked the halter off her breasts, which were not large and looked like they had been squashed flat. She had small but very hard nipples. Bandu pulled the leather skirt down her long muscular thighs. A thong of leather under this was tied between her legs. Pulling it off, she revealed her pubis, its hair as black and curly as the hair on her head. Whether naturally or not, her pubic hair did not extend on to her labia, which — Melinda could see between her thighs — pursed together.

'Now,' she said, sitting on the edge of the bed. 'This is secret. You understand. Secret.' She looked into Melinda's eyes. The dark brown irises were surrounded by cream, not white.

'Yes, mistress.' Obviously Bandu did not have the Emperor's permission for this escapade.

'If not, it is worse for you.'

'Yes, mistress.'

Melinda looked at Bandu's naked body and felt a

surge of desire. The ebony black skin was smooth and had a sheen to it like silk. She wanted to touch it, to stroke it and feel it against her.

'Lie back,' Bandu said, her voice no longer threatening.

Melinda had knelt on the bed. Now she lay on her back as Bandu knelt beside her.

'Open your legs.'

Again Melinda obeyed. Bandu dipped her head. She kissed Melinda's thighs one after the other then stared for a moment at her hairless sex. She moved her mouth and kissed it right at the top of Melinda's labia, her tongue searching out her clitoris. As she did this she moved round, her hands gripping Melinda's legs, until she was kneeling between them. Then she hoisted Melinda's legs up into the air and back over her body, pressing them into her breasts so Melinda was doubled up and the long slit of her sex was completely exposed.

Holding her legs behind the knees, Hadrian's mouth kissed Melinda's labia, darting out her tongue to feel for her clitoris again and then circling the entrance to her sex before plunging inside. Bandu's tongue seemed to be as large as everything else about her. It lapped up into Melinda's silky niche, provoking an immediate response. This had all happened so suddenly and unexpectedly that Melinda's sex was dry. Now, as Bandu's tongue invaded her, a flood of juices rushed to remedy that.

Bandu pulled her tongue out and tested it against the little ring of muscles at Melinda's anus. They gave way and she penetrated there, too, making Melinda gasp. Then her tongue travelled up again, parting the top of the labia and settling on the nut of her clitoris. Her tongue was hard and strong, stronger than any

Melinda could remember. It started by drumming against her, then pushed her clit up and down. In seconds, Melinda's body tensed, the engine of her orgasm starting so quickly that it took her by surprise. As Bandu's tongue stroked against her with a relentless rhythm she felt herself accelerating towards her climax so fast she had no control. The powerful hands of the black woman pressing under her knees and holding her legs against her body, plus the feeling of her own nipples against her legs, all added to her excitement.

Her mind filled with images. She remembered her rider's cock sliding into her, she remembered the Emperor's spunk jetting out from her hand the night before. She looked down between her thighs and could just see, in the narrow gap, the black woman's head working on her, her pink tongue – so pink in contrast to her ebony black face – licking at her eagerly. Melinda's body tensed, a wave of sensation broke over her; she felt another rush of juices flooding from her vagina, and then she was there, thrown over the brink, wallowing in the feelings that shuddered through her nerves.

Bandu dipped her mouth as she felt Melinda quiver, and used her tongue to lap up the product of her sex, savouring the taste and feeling her own sex churn, her own orgasm stirring, her own need asserting itself.

As the last tremors of Melinda's climax shook through her body, the ebony-coloured woman sat up, folding Melinda's legs back on to the bed and caressing her lightly. She looked into Melinda's eyes and a strange expression flitted over her face, a smile of affection that Melinda had never seen before.

Quickly, Bandu swung her big black thigh over

Melinda's face, so her knees were either side of Melinda's shoulders and she was facing her feet.

'Eat me.' The tone of menace had returned. 'Make it good.'

She remained on her haunches, savouring the moment, looking down at the white body she had lusted after since the first moment she had seen it chained to the stone column. Many slaves had passed through her hands but none, she thought, were quite as perfect as this one, her jade green eyes and soft feminine face expressing an attitude of submission like none she had seen. She had rarely been tempted to take the risk before but now the opportunity had presented itself and she already knew Melinda was worth it. Judging from the way her body felt already, the way it had responded to feeling the slave's thick labia and liquid sex, and remembering their previous encounter, she would not be disappointed. Slowly she lowered herself on to Melinda's mouth, her sex throbbing in anticipation.

Melinda stared up between Bandu's black thighs. Her sex, by contrast to the colour of the flesh that framed it, seemed to be like an exotic orchid of scarlet reds and delicate pinks. It was already wet, her inner labia glistening, the mouth of her sex pursed and open, a ragged scarlet gash. As it descended, Melinda raised her head to kiss it, kissing it like a mouth, squirming her lips against the hairless black labia. Pressed against Bandu's flesh her own seemed pale and ghostly white.

Bandu pushed her sex down until Melinda's head rested back on the bed. She kneaded her own breasts mercilessly, squeezing them with her strong hands and pinching her nipples. She wanted to feel the wrench of pain as she felt Melinda's tongue pushing gently into her scarlet sex, then tracing all around the rim, as if testing its elasticity, as if seeing how far it could be stretched. Then it probed deeper.

But Bandu was in no mood for subtlety.

'Clit,' she ordered, moving back and pulling Melinda's tongue from her sex.

Melinda obeyed. She separated the labia and found her lozenge-shaped clit. She sucked it hard and felt Bandu shudder. Almost immediately she felt one, then two, fingers sliding into her own sex. She gasped. Bandu squirmed down on her mouth, her powerful muscles crushing Melinda's head back on to the bed. She rammed her fingers into Melinda's sex, not for Melinda's benefit but for her own, wanting to feel them surrounded by tight silky-wet flesh, wanting to feel the throbbing heat of Melinda's vagina.

She wriggled her bottom from side to side as Melinda desperately tried to keep her tongue on her clitoris, fighting for air as her nose and mouth were pressed hard against Bandu's pliant sex.

'Yes.' Melinda's tongue pressed Bandu's clitoris as if it were a button that opened the gates to a flood of pleasure. Bandu pushed down hard, knowing she was hurting Melinda, knowing she couldn't breath. She wanted to feel Melinda panting and gasping against her sex, and knew she would not take her tongue away no matter what. She had been trained that way. Melinda was a slave; at this very moment, *her* slave. The idea thrilled her. She had seen the Emperor and his guests using and abusing the slaves in the villa. Now it was Bandu's turn.

Melinda was squirming, the black woman's body rigid, unyielding, the fingers inside her as hard as steel. She tried to keep her tongue hard against Bandu's clit, hoping it would bring her off, hoping that she would then relax.

And she did. Suddenly, as though hit by lightning, Bandu's body locked, every muscle stretched. Her nerves screamed as one, the touch and taste and sight of the beautiful slave combined with the awesome sense of power and the feeling that this was stolen pleasure, like food filched from a rich man's table. Which of all these emotions took her over the edge Bandu did not know, but her body pitched and tossed on a sea of sensation – rocking on Melinda's face, pawing at her body, squirming to get every last ounce of pleasure – before Bandu felt the throes slacken and the hard muscle melt to soft compliance again.

Eventually, and without a word, Bandu got off the bed. As Melinda gulped in lungfuls of air, she disappeared through a door which led to a bathroom.

Melinda sat up, her body wet with sweat. She heard running water and the sound of Bandu moving about. She tried to collect her thoughts, her body still trembling from her own orgasm. A noise like the crack of a hammer hitting a plank of wood, hollow and dull, reverberated from the bathroom, and was immediately followed by the sound of a body falling to the floor.

'Melinda!' Hadrian bounded out of the bathroom, the baseball bat in his hand looking incongruous among all the Roman artefacts, as did his trousers and shirt.

'Hadrian!' Melinda had been taken completely by surprise.

'Quick, we've got to tie her up. She's strong. I think I only stunned her.'

Melinda jumped off the bed and they both ran into the bathroom. The room was small, with no more than a cast-iron bath and two taps – of modern design – in one corner. Bandu's naked body lay face down on the white ceramic floor. She was already beginning to stir.

'We've got to find something to tie her up with.'

'You stay here.' Melinda ran back into the bedroom. There was nothing in the chest by the bed so she dashed out into the corridor. There were several rooms identical to Bandu's bedroom but none produced any suitable material. The fourth room was larger and had a wide three-door cupboard set into one of the walls. The first door she opened revealed a treasure trove of chains, leather harnesses, ropes and gags, as well as whips and tawses and some devices Melinda did not recognise, presumably all placed there for a guest who wished to entertain a slave in the comfort of his or her own room.

Grabbing some lengths of rope, Melinda ran to the door. Then she remembered the gags and thought one of those would be useful too. She returned to the cupboard to collect one and, at the same time, added a leather blindfold to her haul.

Back in the bedroom, Bandu looked as though she was about to regain consciousness. Hadrian was standing over her with the baseball bat raised.

'I was just about to hit her again.'

Dropping to her knees, Melinda wrapped a rope around Bandu's ankles, while Hadrian managed to pull her arms behind her back and tie her wrists.

'Got to do it tighter. The longer she takes to escape, the longer we'll have to get clear of this place.'

They tied her elbows together and roped her knees, checking that all the knots were secure. Melinda turned her head and forced the gag between her lips, buckling it tightly at the back of her head. This had the effect of bringing Bandu round. She began to writhe. In minutes, her eyes were fully open and she was using her considerable strength to struggle against the ropes. She raised her legs and pounded on the floor with her feet, making a racket that seemed to reverberate around the villa.

'That's no good,' Hadrian said. 'She'll raise the alarm as soon as they get back.'

Melinda took the blindfold and pulled it over Bandu's eyes despite her efforts to shake it off. But being in darkness did not stop the black woman's movements. She bounced her body up and down on the floor, making an even greater din. If they were anywhere in the house, she would soon have the rest of the Nubians running to the rescue.

'Quick,' Melinda said, taking hold of Bandu's feet. 'I've got an idea.' She began dragging the Nubian out of the bathroom, remembering something she'd seen in the guest room. Hadrian helped. Even with both of them it was a struggle, Bandu trying to kick them at every opportunity. They slid her through the bedroom and out into the corridor.

'There.' Melinda indicated the fourth room along.

Breathlessly, not daring to stop, they tugged and shoved the tightly bound package of Bandu's body down the corridor and into the guest room. At any minute they expected one of the other Nubians to appear; then the whole escape plan would be over, and the Emperor would never allow his son such freedom again.

But no one appeared. Panting and sweating, they manoeuvred the black woman into the guest room and closed the door, sinking to the bed to catch their breath. But they could not rest long. With terrific strength, their captive started to bounce herself back towards the door, the wooden floor making a great deal more noise than the tiled bathroom had done.

'What are we going to do?' Hadrian asked, as he pulled Bandu back.

'There, look . . .' Melinda pointed to a pulley hanging from one of the wooden beams that ran across the ceiling. Like the cupboard full of equipment, it was obviously provided for the convenience of a guest who wished to bind and whip a slave. The rope from the pulley was tied off on a metal cleat on the side wall.

Taking a rope from the cupboard, having already used up all the ones she had taken out originally, Melinda threaded it around the bindings on Bandu's ankles, then pulled them up and tied them securely to her wrists so her legs were bent backwards.

Hadrian had slackened the rope on the pulley, letting it out enough to be able to reach Bandu. Melinda took it and wound it round the loops she had made, binding her wrists and ankles together. As soon as this was done, they both went to the other end and began to tug the rope back through the pulley. Slowly, relentlessly at first, Bandu's body was dragged across the floor until it was under the pulley. Even more slowly they managed to hoist it into the air, Melinda and Hadrian tugging together inch by inch, until the hog-tied woman was hanging face down three feet above the floor. As much as she tried to writhe and bounce, now there was nothing for her to hit to make any sort of noise.

Her body twisted around in mid-air. She tried to scream but the gag prevented all but a muffled groan.

'Wonderful,' Hadrian said, delighted with Melinda's invention.

'But if this room is occupied they'll find her when they get back,' Melinda warned.

'But probably not until after the feast. And by then . . .'

'What?'

'Whoever's in this room might think it's a little gift from my father. Come on, we've got to hurry . . .' He caught Melinda's hand and pulled her out of the room, though not before she'd straightened the sheet where they'd sat down and checked nothing else was out of place.

Melinda started down the corridor but he stopped her.

'No. This way.'

He led her back to Bandu's room. He took a small pair of wire-cutters from his pocket, knelt at her feet and cut through the gold chain that held the electronic tag on her ankle. He picked it up and placed it under the pillow on Bandu's bed.

'Now we go,' he said, picking up the baseball bat from the bathroom.

Stealthily they half-walked and half-ran through the corridors to the main staircase. Just as they were about to descend, Melinda glanced out of the window. Across the courtyard, a procession was being led by the Emperor on a white horse, guests, slaves and overseers all following behind. A babble of excited conversation floated up to the villa. The group was heading straight for the main entrance.

'Quick.' Melinda remembered a window on the other side of the house by the Emperor's bedroom. There was a large and mature tree outside it, which they could climb down.

Running full-pelt now, they got to the window which had been left open. There was a branch about three feet from the sill which was strong enough to take both their weights.

Hadrian helped her out, holding her hands until her feet were firmly on the branch, then followed her.

They both shimmied down the tree, Melinda scratching her naked flesh on the rough bark. They were in the clearing at the far side of the house, away from the returning entourage, though they could still hear all the voices.

Taking her hand, Hadrian ran with Melinda to the outer wall. They didn't dare risk the main gate, as they would undoubtedly be seen. Fortunately, there was a stack of logs against part of the wall. They ran to it and Hadrian helped Melinda up until she could get her hands on to the top of the stone and pull herself up and over it. She dropped to the ground on the other side, waiting anxiously for Hadrian.

Suddenly she heard a crash of logs. The log pile must have collapsed. With bated breath she waited, knowing he could not call out to her for fear of being heard. She'd hoped the noise hadn't already alerted somebody. To her relief, a hand appeared on top of the wall, which was then followed by a second. Hadrian hauled himself up and vaulted to the ground.

'Near thing,' he whispered, as they ran into the trees beyond the clearing, welcoming their shade and cover.

Taking her hand, Hadrian orientated himself and ran across the grass into the trees. There was no path and the undergrowth was thick and spiky, which made Melinda cry out.

'Can you make it?' he asked.

'Yes, it's OK. Keep going.'

Ignoring the thistles and brambles that stabbed at her feet and legs, Melinda followed as Hadrian led the way. After a few minutes they reached a path and he started to run at a trot. Five minutes later she saw a shape among the trees.

'We're here,' he announced. A pile of big, leafy

branches had been cut and stacked in a small clearing to conceal a fairly large object. He began pulling them away and Melinda saw, underneath, a bright-red American four-wheel drive Jeep with a covered top.

'Come on.' He was holding the passenger door open. She scrambled in. After so long in the villa, with evidence of the twentieth century carefully concealed, the interior of the Jeep was a considerable shock, like moving through two thousand years in ten minutes. For a moment she gazed around all the glimmering metal and dials, switches and knobs, as though transported to Aladdin's cave. She glanced into the back where, judging from the ruffled sleeping-bag and cans of food, it was obvious Hadrian had spent the night.

Pulling the rest of the branches away, Hadrian climbed into the driving seat and started the engine. It made a noise like thunder.

'They'll hear . . .' she said.

'No. No one came last night and they're making a lot more noise now with the banquet.'

He slammed the engine into gear and, driving as quietly as possible, set off through the trees. There was no track for cars but it was possible to pick a way back through the undergrowth; the twin tracks the tyres had made on the way in were clearly visible. Slowly, the number of trees lessened and they were able to pick up speed, going faster and faster and getting further and further away from the villa.

After fifteen minutes, the Jeep broke through into the open. There was a short incline, on top of which was a tarmac road. Two cars swept by, a smart Lancia and a Mercedes, followed by an eight-wheeled truck. Melinda was back in the twentieth century.

Ten

'There's a track suit in the back. And I've got you some clothes in my bag. We'll get you everything else you need in the morning.'

Melinda found a nylon holdall on the back seat. It contained a blue sweatshirt-type top and trousers with an elasticated waist and ankles. There was also a pair of white trainers.

They were on a main road and it was dark. Other drivers may well have caught a glimpse of a naked woman struggling into the track suit as they passed the Jeep going in the opposite direction.

'We're going to a hotel,' Hadrian said.

It felt odd to be clothed again after so long naked or semi-naked. It was the first time Melinda's sex had been closely covered since her unceremonious arrival at the villa. The lining of the track suit was fleecy and warm and felt good against her skin. The trainers were too big for her.

'Sorry, I didn't know your size.'

She hadn't said a word to him since their escape and they had been driving for more than an hour. She felt alienated and disorientated. For the first time in almost a year she was outside any order – not under the protection of the OIM or the surrogate Master, the Emperor. She had, at least temporarily, regained her own will. She could ask Hadrian to stop the car, or get her a drink or something to eat, or any one of a hundred other things. She could comb her own hair and put on her make-up and look in a mirror for as long as she liked. She even knew what time it was, courtesy of the clock on the Jeep's dashboard. She was, once again, a person, not an object; she was not surprised to discover she did not care for it at all.

It had to be endured. She knew that. She had to manipulate Hadrian into getting what she wanted. That involved behaving as normally as she could. From his point of view, her being a slave was a silly game she had played at the behest of his father, who he probably thought was mad – and quite rightly so. He wanted her as a person not as a slave, and fondly imagined that his sexual infatuation with her was love. He wanted to do everything a couple in love would do.

Melinda's agenda was rather different. Her first priority was to get in touch with the OIM. Everything followed from that. She hoped she could find a way not to leave Hadrian brokenhearted.

She found it difficult to talk. After so long being allowed to speak only in reply to a question, initiating a conversation proved impossible. Fortunately Hadrian appeared to be content to drive in silence, occasionally reaching out and dropping his hand on to her leg and squeezing it gently, perhaps taking her quietness for exhaustion.

They were driving on a road that wound down from some fairly steep hills, the ones Melinda remembered they had climbed during the kidnap. When they reached the plane below, the roads became straighter, and after an hour or so they reached a small town, its main street busy, the cafés in its central piazza full of people taking coffee and brandy in the balmy night air.

There was only one small three-storey hotel, a crumbling nineteenth-century façade with ornate double entrance doors from a later period of art deco, brass handles and finger-plates highly polished. Hadrian parked on the street in front of the hotel, just managing to squeeze the big Jeep in between a Fiat and a Ford.

'Is this far enough?' Melinda asked anxiously.

'We'll be safe here.'

'Do you think they'll come after us?'

'If they do, there's no way they could know which direction we've come. There must be fifty towns in a hundred-mile radius. It's impossible, believe me.'

'I don't want to go back there.'

Hadrian walked round to the passenger door and opened it for her. Despite his reassurances, Melinda felt uneasy. Life at the villa had been as exciting as it had at any of the other establishments she had been sent to, but she definitely didn't want to go back. The Emperor had treated her well, better than some Masters, but that was when he had no cause to doubt her loyalty. His attitude was certain to be less sympathetic if he caught her: with his megalomania there was no telling what he'd do. Melinda shuddered.

Hadrian took a small suitcase from the back of the Jeep; they walked up the steps and through the art deco doors. Within minutes they were being shown into an ancient lift by an even older man who had insisted on carrying the case. He escorted them down a faded corridor on the third floor – the carpet threadbare, the paint on the walls flaking – to a battered panelled door, its varnish cracked and crazed.

The bedroom was large, with a big double mattress

in a cast-iron bedstead. The furniture was all mahogany. A big wardrobe, the chest of drawers and bedside tables were all decorated with little yellow bunches of marquetry. Heavy velvet curtains, that had once been a deep red but now were a dirty brown, draped the large window that overlooked the square. Melinda noticed that the room did not have a telephone.

'Not too bad,' Hadrian said, bouncing on the bed. The room smelt of musk and felt damp, but the sheets on the bed were white and spotlessly clean.

Melinda inspected the bathroom. Incongruously, it was lined with sheets of thick grey marble, with a large tub and double hand basins, and was as luxurious as any to be found in a five-star hotel.

Hadrian opened his case. 'I had to guess your size,' he said. He threw a black bra, panties and a suspender belt on the bed, all expensive, lacy silk. There were two pairs of stockings in grey and black, plus two pairs of tights in skin tones, as well as two pairs of shoes, black high heels and low-heeled loafers. He had bought a simple, black shift dress in silk and a more practical shirtwaister in cream.

'Put something on and we'll go down to dinner. You must be starving. I am.'

Whether out of consideration for her or through nerves, he made no attempt to touch her. But he watched avidly as she pulled off the track suit and went into the bathroom. She did not close the bathroom door after her, not wanting him to feel excluded. Hadrian remained sitting on the bed.

When she had washed and dried herself, she came back into the bedroom. She picked up the black bra and fed the straps over her shoulders. The lacy cups were a good fit for her breasts. As she clipped the bra into place behind her back, its support and constriction felt strange. The last time she had worn anything like this was the blue satin halter she had worn when she was tied to the Emperor's bed.

'Do you shave?' Hadrian asked. He was still sitting on the bed, his eyes rooted to her hairless pubis as she stepped into the black panties and pulled them up over her hips.

'I was made to,' she replied. It was all she could do to stop herself from adding 'Master'.

'It's nice. I like it. Would you shave for me?'

'Of course.' She wanted to say, of course Master, I'll do anything for you Master, don't you realise that, but she didn't. 'I'll do anything you want, Hadrian,' she said instead.

She saw a bulge growing in the front of his trousers as he got up to use the bathroom.

He had remembered a hairbrush for her and a little plastic case of make-up. She took them and stood in front of the mirror that hung on the wall above the chest of drawers. Her face stared back at her. She looked into her jade green eyes and saw, among all the feelings they struggled to express, one overriding emotion: fear. She was frightened. The whole situation was frightening: she had to cope with decisions, had to decide what to do – everything from how to make up and comb her hair to how to get in touch with the OIM and deal with Hadrian. She had wanted none of this. She thought of Sophia, thought of the excitement and desire the woman created in her. How wonderful it would be to find her again, to be taken to her home, perhaps to be bound tightly in a neat ball so she could do nothing but obey.

She brushed her hair and applied eye-liner, shadow and a dark red lipstick; Melinda tried not to think of anything except what she had to do.

They went down to dinner in the restaurant. The black high heels were two sizes too big for her and Melinda had to walk slowly. As they walked through the reception area she noticed a telephone booth in the corner.

Hadrian was attentive and expansive over dinner, and, as they ate pasta followed by grilled veal, he talked excitedly of their escape. He told her how he had watched her and the other body slaves being taken to the arena, then sneaked back into the house as soon as his father had left with all the guests. He had waited patiently and, from a vantage point on the first floor, had eventually seen the four Nubians and the slaves return.

The most difficult part was getting into Bandu's bathroom. He had watched Melinda being led into the house and had hidden as they had passed him in an upstairs corridor. With Bandu's weight and strength he had calculated he wouldn't stand a chance if he just marched into the room and confronted her face to face. He needed the element of surprise. The room next to the bathroom had a window out on to a small ledge. He'd crawled along it and found, luckily, that the bathroom window was open. There he'd waited behind the door. As soon as Bandu had bent over to run her bath he'd hit her with the baseball bat.

Melinda looked around nervously throughout the meal, expecting the Emperor, or especially the avenging Bandu, to come charging through the doors. But no one came.

As Hadrian talked, she devised her plan of action. Hopefully he would be a heavy sleeper and she could sneak out of bed and get downstairs to the telephone booth. She had no idea how to contact the OIM.

209

They would hardly be listed in the telephone directory, and she had none of the names of her Masters, let alone their addresses. The only name she did know was that of her first Master, Walter Hammerton, the man who had initiated her into the organisation. She would have to get his number and ring him. She knew the name of his company and knew he had an office in Rome. She only hoped his office was manned at night time.

They bothed refused dessert and coffee, and Hadrian signed the bill. As they got up, Hadrian took her hand and kissed the tips of her fingers. 'I've talked too much,' he said.

'No, it's my fault. I . . . I've lost the habit of . . . I don't seem to be able to . . .' She couldn't explain how difficult she found it to make conversation.

'It's all right,' he said. 'You've been through a lot.'

They walked down to the lift hand in hand. As soon as he'd closed the double grilles and the lift began to clang noisily upward, he pulled her into his arms and kissed her full on the mouth, pressing his tongue between her lips and letting her feel his erection growing against her belly.

'So exciting . . .' he whispered, as the lift's arrival signalled the end of the kiss. Hadrian looked like a little boy about to play with a new toy for the first time.

He unlocked the bedroom door and kissed her again the moment they got inside. She watched with relief as he bolted it from the inside.

'So exciting . . .' he repeated, running his hands over her body in the black dress, his cock pressing on the front of his trousers.

Melinda dropped to her knees and immediately pulled down the zip of his flies. She fished inside and extracted his cock from his boxer shorts, closing her mouth on it and sucking it in deeply until the material of his trousers was brushing her lips and his glans was tight against the back of her throat.

He moaned.

Remembering what had happened the first time, she withdrew her mouth, kissed the tip of his cock lightly and stood up. She had to be careful. She wanted to make sure Hadrian had a good time, a time he would never forget – an experience that would make him sleep dreamlessly and deeply.

'Let me get ready for you,' she said. She picked up the suspender belt and the pack of black stockings and walked into the bathroom, this time shutting the door behind her.

She felt disorientated again, not used to a man who did not order her what to do. At the same time, she wanted to please Hadrian as a way of repaying him for what he had done.

Melinda peeled off the dress and pulled the black panties down her slender legs. She sat on the edge of the bath, unwrapped the cellophane packet and extracted the stockings. Slowly, being very careful not to snag them, she rolled them up over her legs and on to her thighs. She wrapped the lacy black suspender belt around her body. It had a broad, long waistband that covered half her navel. She clipped the suspenders into the tops of the stockings at the front and sides, adjusting them so they were held taut.

She stood up, allowing herself to glance in the mirror that she had so far deliberately avoided. The black of the bra and the suspender belt bit tightly into her flesh. She shivered slightly. The underwear reminded her of bondage, the harnesses that had so often been strapped to her body to constrict it in a hundred different ways. She felt her sex moisten.

Though the high heels were too big for her, she put them back on. They firmed and shaped her legs, increasing the distinct pout of her bottom where the top of her thighs tucked into her buttocks. Opening the bathroom door, she walked back into the bedroom.

Hadrian was lying naked on the bed. His cock was erect but he was not playing with it, perhaps fearing he may not be able to control his ejaculation again.

Melinda stood in front of him, her legs open, arms akimbo, her sex perfectly framed by the black lace of the suspender belt and the smooth, shiny nylon of the stockings.

'What would you like me to do, Master?' She used the word deliberately. It made her feel comfortable, at ease: it also made her feel incredibly aroused. She hoped it would not annoy Hadrian.

It didn't.

'Touch yourself,' he said, not at all tentatively.

She slid one hand down between her legs while the other squeezed her breast under the bra.

'You'll do anything, won't you?'

'Yes, Master, anything for you.' How good it felt to say those words again.

'But what do *you* want?' He was staring at the way her fingers had parted the lips of her sex to reveal her clitoris. He could see she was already wet.

'I want what I am told to do, Master.' It was the absolute truth.

'Come over here.' She could see the total fascination in his face. She walked to the bed without moving her hands from her sex or her breast.

He stared into her eyes, then put his hand out to touch the nylon welt of the stocking. He rubbed his palm against it, then moved his hand higher on to her naked flesh as if contrasting the texture of the two.

'Take your hand away,' he said, then changed his mind. 'No, open for me.'

Melinda opened her legs wider and used both hands to hold her labia apart. He was not satisfied by that.

'Get on the bed,' he ordered, slipping easily into the role of Master.

She lay across the big bed, opened her stockinged legs wide and bent her knees, the high heels digging into the bed and creasing the sheets. She spread her labia apart as Hadrian knelt beside her, looking down into her sex. He could see the whitish pink of her clitoris, the scarlet opening of her vagina and the corrugated hole of her anus. He studied them all intently. His cock produced a tear of fluid.

'Do you like it, Master?' She shouldn't have spoken. It was against the rules, but Hadrian would not complain and she needed to guide him.

'Yes,' he said, under his breath.

'And this?'

She turned over on to her stomach and raised her bottom into the air. Her forehead pressed into the sheet, her knees bent and her legs spread; her sex moved even closer to his face.

'Yes.'

He watched as she snaked a hand up between her legs and held her labia apart so he could see more clearly. The inner flesh glistened.

'Get your belt, Master, from your trousers.'

'What?'

'I want it, Master.' It was true; she did, though it felt so strange using the word 'I' again. Over the past months 'I' had been deliberately eliminated from her life.

Like a man in a trance, Hadrian got to his feet,

walked to the small armchair upholstered in a faded flowery print where he had left his trousers, and pulled the thin leather belt from the loops around the waistband.

As he came back to the side of the bed, Melinda wriggled her pert round arse from side to side, leaving him in no doubt as to what she wanted him to do.

'You want this?' There was incredulity in his voice, but fascination, too.

'Oh yes, Master. From you, Master.'

Hadrian touched her bottom with his hand. He slipped his finger into her labia and felt her heat and wetness. Her excitement was obvious. So was his own. His cock felt like a bone; he could never remember it being so hard.

He raised his arm in the air, whipped the belt back and slashed it across Melinda's buttocks. It was a perfect strike, right across the meat of her bottom. She gasped, the familiar surge of pain followed by the equally familiar flush of pleasure.

'Oh yes, Master, yes.' She wanted him to hear her pleasure as well as see it.

'Yes?' he asked, slashing the thin belt down again. 'Yes?'

'Oh, Master.' A third stroke followed the second almost instantly. Three red weals appeared, crisscrossing each other. Melinda felt her body responding to the unique pleasure that only pain could induce. She managed to glance sideways at Hadrian, to make sure this was turning him on, too; her pleasure, after all, was secondary. She only had to glimpse the state of his cock to know that it was.

'More?' But before she could answer, he delivered a fourth and fifth stroke, then threw the belt aside.

She had no need to guide him now. He knew exactly what he wanted. Leaping up on to the bed, he knelt between her legs and pushed his cock into her labia. He found the opening to her sex and sunk home up to the hilt. He moaned, his navel pressed against the heat of the red weals he had created, his hands on top of her hips, the silky black lace under his palms.

For a moment he did not move. Melinda feared he was not going to be able to control himself as she felt his cock throbbing urgently inside her.

Hadrian felt the same. As he looked down at her back, sloping away from him, bisected by the tight suspenders, he thought he was going to come. The excitement he had felt as he'd slashed the belt against Melinda's buttocks was extreme. He loved the way the flesh vibrated, and the sound as the leather thwacked the flesh; he loved the red weals that marked her soft skin. More than that, he loved the excitement it created in her, the gasps of pleasure that escaped her lips, the little squirming movements she made to fan the heat produced by the weals with a draught of air. He suddenly thought of his father and his father's slaves; the idea did not seem so preposterous after all.

He held himself completely still, feeling his spunk pumping in his cock, imagining at any moment that it would spew out of him. But it didn't. Miraculously, he seemed to be gaining control, as he had before with Melinda at the villa.

He tentatively moved his cock out and in again, feeling Melinda's wet sex clinging to him. He reached forward and unclipped the back of her bra, then pushed the cups off to replace them with his hands.

'You're so hard, Master,' she said.

'Yes, I am.' He began to stroke to and fro more confidently, pinching at her large nipples and kneading the pliant flesh of her breasts, feeling more and more confident that he would not disgrace himself. His cock was covered with her juices, which ran down his shaft and over his big hairy balls as they brushed against her bottom.

There was no danger of him coming now, until he wanted to. He felt strong and able and masculine. He would have liked to stop to pick up the belt again – watch as he delivered more strokes across that wonderful round arse, watch as more red weals appeared on her flesh – but there would be lots of time for that later. He had thought of Melinda as his lover but it was becoming increasingly easy to imagine how good it would be to have her as his slave. She was trained to it, as his father had said. Trained to obey, trained to submit.

He slowed his cock. He had thought of something else he wanted, something he had never tried with a woman. Slipping his cock from her vagina, he found the little bud of her anus with no difficulty. Instantly he felt her react, squirming her bottom back at him as if to say she wanted it.

'Oh, Master.' The excitement in her voice was obvious.

Encouraged, he pushed forward. The ring of sphincter was tense but as he pushed forward he felt it relax. The wetness from her sex made the first penetration effortless.

'Oh, Master.' Her voice was husky with passion.

'So tight,' he said. 'So tight, isn't it?' He pushed forward, filling her rear passage with his cock.

'Yes, Master.'

'Buggering you.' The word excited him.

'Yes, Master.' Melinda could hardly get the words out, her body was so overwhelmed with sensation.

'You want it, don't you?'

'Yes, Master.'

He bucked his hips to and fro. He had never done it before, there was so much he had never done. It was exciting but he remained in control.

Not for much longer, however.

Melinda was still in the same position, her forehead resting on the sheet, her buttocks raised. She could see him kneeling behind her, see his balls swinging back and forth. She reached back with one hand until her fingers were nestling against her labia. Her clitoris was hot and swollen. She stroked it gently for a second but stopped, the waves of pleasure this created were too distracting. Her aim was to please Hadrian, her own feelings were unimportant.

The tip of her finger found the entrance to her vagina, made smaller by his cock in her other passage. With one, then two, fingers she widened the opening, then pushed inside. Almost immediately she heard Hadrian moan. She pushed deeper, feeling her own silky wet flesh give way. On the top and sides of her vagina she could feel the spongy elasticity of her sex, along the bottom the hardness of his cock. Stretching the tendons of her fingers, she ran them up and down the shaft. She felt him stop his movement, wanting to feel the extraordinary sensation of being touched while still impaled inside her.

Melinda could feel his cock throbbing again as it had when he'd first plunged it into her. She wanted to make him come like this, it was an experience he would never forget. Supporting herself on her forehead, she snaked her other hand back between her legs. His cock was pressed deep into her body but his balls hung loose. Her fingers closed on his ball sac.

'God,' he cried loudly.

She jiggled his balls, then pulled the whole sac down sharply.

'Come, Master,' she encouraged.

And he did. As if she had turned on a switch to open the floodgates of his cock, he spasmed and a stream of white-hot spunk shot out of him into the tight confines of her rear, too much stimulation to resist any longer, too many new experiences to assimilate. His body shook violently.

Then something occurred which Melinda had not expected. Her own body convulsed, the twin invaders – his cock and her hand – too much to ignore. The pain from the whipping and the cock in her anus had long since turned to pulses of hot bubbling pleasure, but, like the sound of a double bass, were deep and resonant but in the background. Now, as she felt his spunk lashing into her most private of places, they suddenly shouted in the foreground, too. Without consciously thinking about what she was doing, she slipped her hand from his balls to her clitoris, pushing the little nut of nerves from side to side with no subtlety.

He had recovered sufficiently to realise what she was doing. Taking his hand from her hip, he slid it around her navel and down between her legs, replacing her fingers on her clit with his own.

'Let me,' he hissed.

His rhythm was the same. She slipped her fingers out of her sex, needing nothing else but the pressure of his finger.

'Oh, Master,' she said. Her orgasm had taken control, the waves of sensation coming quicker and quicker as he bucked his still hard erection in her arse and pressed her clitoris from side to side with all his strength. 'Master.' She repeated the word as her orgasm erupted, a wall of crimson flooding through her mind as her body locked rigid and her eyes screwed shut.

He had made her come. He was a natural Master. She knew he was not just playing a part. He had enjoyed it, revelled in it, wanted it.

As his cock slipped from her body, slimed with his own spunk, and he lay back on the bed, she had the feeling that something had changed irrevocably between them. He was no longer infatuated with her as he had been before. He wanted her, and wanted to be with her. Now he realised that what she had done at the villa was not a game. He understood now what it meant when she said she was a slave.

She got up off the bed and began unclipping the stockings, feeling again the strangeness of not being told what to do.

'Tell me about the OIM,' he said, as he propped himself up against the pillows.

'What do you want to know?'

'Everything.'

'What did your father tell you?'

'That it is a society of very rich men and women who have the facilities to indulge a similar interest . . .'

'Well . . .'

Melinda told him what she knew, concentrating on the general principles, on the big houses and the anonymity and the absolute need to obey. Her voice soon became hoarse. It was a long time since she'd spoken so much.

'And membership can be inherited? That's what my father said,' he added.

'Yes, but not in your father's case.'

'Why not?'

'Hadrian, your father's no longer a member. They threw him out because he broke their rules.'

'What?'

'He runs the villa on the same principles but it's no longer anything to do with the OIM.'

'He told me they were all fools, that he wanted to start his own organisation.'

'He's been kidnapping girls from them, including me.'

'God.'

'It's true.'

'That means...' He didn't finish the sentence. Hadrian had seen a dream opening up in front of him. Melinda had shown him what it would be like to be a Master, what an aphrodisiac power could be. He had begun to appreciate the advantages of being a Master. But after what he had done, his father was unlikely to let him back into the villa for a long time.

'It means you'll have to go it alone,' Melinda said.

'When I'm twenty-one I'm going to have a huge inheritance. You can teach me. Like you've done tonight. I can join the OIM in my own right.'

'Yes, Master,' she said softly.

He smiled. 'I like that, I shall be my own Master.'

Exhausted now after the events of the day, they lay side by side in the double bed; soon Melinda heard Hadrian's heavy breathing ring out through the room. She found it difficult not to fall asleep herself after everything that had happened, but knew she must remain awake at all costs. She had escaped the villa, part one of her plan was complete, but now she must escape Hadrian, too. Despite her feelings of gratitude to him, her duty was clear. First of all, she had to get back to the OIM; second, she had to try to give them a clue to the location of the villa so they could rescue the other slaves, like Mollie, who had been kidnapped.

After half an hour she rolled off the bed, waiting to see if she'd roused Hadrian before walking to the door. His breathing remained unchanged. Stealthily, she picked up the shirtwaister and the loafers and stepped out into the corridor. The door lock clicked as she closed the door but she heard no noise from inside the room to indicate that it had woken Hadrian.

Standing naked in the corridor, she slipped into the dress and shoes and walked down the narrow winding staircase. She did not want to use the lift because of its noise; an irrational fear, as their room was well away from the lift shaft.

Though it was late, the bar of the hotel was still busy, and people came and went through the ornate front doors.

There was a man in a smart business suit behind the reception desk. He smiled at her, flashing an array of gleaming white teeth.

'I need a telephone directory for Rome,' she said.

'Certainly, *signorina*.' He reached under the counter and produced a thick book which he handed to her.

'How do I make a call?'

'Give me the number. I get for you. You take over there.' He indicated the telephone booth she had spotted earlier.

Melinda flicked through the directory, found Walter Hammerton's company and reeled off the number. The receptionist wrote it down.

She was about to walk over to the booth when she had an idea. 'I wonder . . .'

'*Si, signorina.*'

'My Italian is not good. There's probably only a

security guard on duty. Do you think you could ask them for the London number of the company?'

'Of course.'

'Then ring that for me?'

'*Si, signorina.*'

'*Grazie.*'

'*Prego.*'

He dialled the number into the phone on the counter top and was soon speaking in rapid-fire Italian. Much to Melinda's relief, the switchboard at the Rome office was manned twenty-four hours a day. He hung up.

'I have the number. I ring now?'

'Please.'

'You take in booth, please.'

She walked over to the booth and shut herself inside, dulling the noise that came from the bar. There was a little padded stool screwed to the floor and she sat down on it. The phone rang almost immediately.

'Hello.'

'Hammerton International.' It was a cultured English voice. 'How may I help you?'

'I need to speak to Walter Hammerton.'

'It's very late.'

'I know. It's urgent and extremely important. I need to have his home number...' Melinda was floundering, trying to think of a way to convince this woman to give her Walter's home number. It would obviously be highly confidential information and not something she'd give out to anyone phoning in the middle of the night. She was having trouble forming words and sentences, let alone trying to think. There was only one hope. If the OIM had alerted Walter to her disappearance, he might realise she would only have one way to contact him and may have briefed his switchboard accordingly.

'I'm afraid I couldn't possibly . . .' the woman was saying.

'I'm from the OIM,' Melinda interrupted.

The woman went silent for a moment.

'Did you say OIM?'

'Yes.'

'Hold the line.'

There was a series of clicks, then a female voice said, 'I think it's her.'

'Melinda?' The voice was deep and sonorous. She swooned when she heard it. After everything she had been through, hearing Walter Hammerton's voice was like reaching a lifeboat in a storm-tossed sea.

'Master.' Tears were welling in her eyes.

'Where are you?'

She read the name and address of the hotel from the poster above the phone.

'Are you in danger?'

She could see Walter's steel blue eyes staring at her hypnotically. She felt a surge of desire.

'No, Master.'

'We will be there in the morning, first thing in the morning. Just walk out of the hotel at eight. By yourself. Everything will be taken care of.'

'Thank you, Master.'

'You did the right thing, Melinda. I'm very proud of you.'

'Thank you, Master.'

'Remember, eight.'

'Yes, Master.'

As the phone went dead, Melinda felt a rush of relief. It was all but over. Soon she would be back where she belonged. She had no more decisions to make, no more plans to concoct.

* * *

Hadrian was still asleep at quarter to eight. Melinda dressed herself in the shirtwaister, deliberating over whether to omit underwear. For a moment she felt a surge of affection for the young boy who had helped her escape. She had used him, of course, but she didn't think he would be too upset at her loss. A new world had opened up for him the night before. If he wanted to spend his fortune on joining the OIM he would be able to do it without her help.

She bent over and kissed his cheek but he did not stir. She wouldn't have worried if he had. She would just have told him she was going outside to get some air.

This time, she did use the lift. As it clanged to a halt on the ground floor the clock above the reception desk struck eight. Melinda was surprised to see the same receptionist on duty who had helped her the night before. She smiled at him as he wished her '*buon giorno*'.

She went to the glass doors and grasped the gleaming handle, knowing as she walked through them she would be in a different world again. She did not hesitate.

The red Jeep had gone. Parked in its place was a large grey van. Standing by the driver's door was a woman dressed entirely in black, tight black leggings, and an equally close-fitting black leotard. She was wearing a floppy-brimmed black hat and high-heeled black boots. The expression on her face showed not a flicker of emotion.

As Melinda walked down the front steps of the hotel, the woman came over to her and took her by the arm, her bony fingers pressing into Melinda's flesh. There were two powerful black cars parked on either side of the van with two burly men in each.

The woman marched Melinda to the back of the

van as the men got out of the black cars and went into the hotel.

'In,' she said, opening one of the van's doors.

The interior of the van was painted black. The woman closed the rear door again and Melinda was plunged into darkness. She heard the driver's door slam and the engine start; she braced herself against the side panel as the van lurched away.

Familiar feelings flooded through Melinda, her will and individuality excised from her with surgical precision, the blackness in the back of the van a welcome sign that she was no longer in control.

After a fifteen-minute drive, the van came to a halt. The back door opened and the woman peered inside. 'Out,' she ordered. 'Give me your dress and shoes. Put these on.' She handed Melinda a pair of plain black panties, the type always used for slaves in transit between Masters.

They were parked in the corner of a field of hay – nothing but hedges and trees for miles.

Melinda stripped off the dress. It was an unusually cold day and the sun was hidden behind scudding clouds.

'Show me your marks,' the woman commanded.

Melinda lifted her breasts towards her chin, revealing two purple squares etched with the letter M. The woman seemed satisfied. Melinda took off her shoes and handed them to the woman and then stepped into the panties, pulling them tightly over her hips.

They waited by the back door of the van. After a few minutes, the distant roar of a helicopter could be heard. It approached rapidly and was soon whipping the grass in the field as it landed near the van.

'You must show them the villa,' the woman said, pulling Melinda by the arm towards the aircraft, stooping as they ran under the whirling rotor blades. The cockpit door opened and Melinda was helped inside. The pilot was a woman. She did not look at Melinda but lifted the helicopter off the moment both women were aboard.

'The hotel first. Try to remember from there.'

As they hovered over the town piazza, Melinda could see three men coming out of the back entrance of the hotel. The one in the middle was Hadrian, being frogmarched by the other two. One of the big black cars had been driven round to the back and Hadrian was bundled inside.

'Which way?' the pilot prompted.

Melinda indicated the road they had driven along to get to the hotel and the pilot followed it. On the ground the two black cars followed the helicopter, which flew low just above the treetops.

Finding the villa was easier than she would have imagined. She remembered they had taken few turns on the road from the hills and it was quite simple to pick out the landmarks. Soon they were up in the hills. Once they encountered the woods, it was more difficult to decide which direction they had taken in the Jeep, they had several false starts, flying over treetops that all looked the same. But suddenly Melinda saw the steep cliff that stuck up almost vertically and immediately directed the pilot to it. From there it was easy to direct them to the villa.

The helicopter banked high once the pilot had noted the position, not wanting to alert the Emperor or anyone else at the villa. The pilot radioed down to the two cars that waited back on the main road and which had been joined by a large truck full of men. The hordes were gathering for another sack of Rome.

* * *

They left Melinda alone. It was the same halfway house and the same room with the long mirror. She was dressed exactly the same as last time she had been in this room, naked but for the plain black nylon panties. The heat had returned, too. Her body was beaded with sweat. It was almost as if the villa and the Emperor had never existed. But she knew they had.

They had allowed her to see Mollie, but not to talk to her, of course. She had seen the Nubians, too, their bodies bound in thick leather straps. Bandu had glared at her; the gag had prevented her expressing the rage Melinda could see in her eyes.

What would happen to the Emperor she had no way of knowing. There were Masters who had establishments – though naturally she had never been to one – serviced entirely by male slaves. Perhaps the man who believed he was the master of all he surveyed was to be shipped to one of them.

Hadrian, she was sure, would not be punished. He had nothing to do with his father's schemes and indeed had helped bring the whole edifice crumbling down. She was sure he would be busy ingratiating himself with the organisation and planning how soon he could become a member.

Slowly, almost without thinking, as the sun began to set and the cell darkened, she slipped her fingers into the front of her panties. She thought of Walter Hammerton and what he had said to her on the phone. She yearned to see him again and to serve him. She felt her body moisten at the thought. She sank to her knees in front of the mirror and watched as her hand moved under the tight black nylon; her finger found her clitoris and rubbed it hard, pressing it against her pubic bone. Her other hand first pinched both her nipples, so hard the feeling would linger, then pushed into the back of the panties, her middle finger testing the hole Hadrian had penetrated the night before. She felt her body throb, her juices gushing, her mind full of images.

Tomorrow she would be sent to Sophia and her new Master. Tomorrow she hoped she would be bound and beaten, and made to obey. But today, she could indulge herself. She was back in the limbo of transit, after all. Tonight, perhaps, someone was watching behind the mirror, someone with greedy narrowed eyes wanting to see her perform.

She rocked her finger against her clit, spreading her knees further apart. She hoped they were all watching, hoped they could all see her fingers working feverishly under the black nylon, penetrating both passages of her body, prodding and probing and provoking herself to pleasure, as she knew she would not be permitted to do again for a very long time.

NEW BOOKS

Coming up from Nexus and Black Lace

Nexus

Underworld by Maria del Rey
February 1995   Price: £4.99   ISBN: 0 352 32971 8
Behind a façade of respectability, a group of wealthy professionals hides a sordid secret: an elite club where they engage in debauched games of master and servant. Pamela, a private eye, has to go undercover to trace a missing lover. But the cover is deep, and she is soon relishing the activities she is meant to be investigating.

Melinda and the Roman by Susanna Hughes
February 1995   Price: £4.99   ISBN: 0 352 32972 6
Melinda's latest home is her strangest yet. In her eccentric Master's villa, everything is exactly as it was in ancient Rome. Slaves carry out their Master's every bidding; discipline is rigorously enforced; and dissolute orgies go on all day and night. Melinda has very little trouble fitting in.

The Handmaidens by Aran Ashe
March 1995   Price: £4.99   ISBN: 0 352 32985 8
Aran Ashe, creator of the legendary Lidir books, is back with a brilliant new series of erotic fantasy novels: the Chronicles of Tormunil. In this, the first book, we meet Sianon and Iroise, young and beautiful serving wenches who seem condemned to a future of absolute obedience and self-denial in the sinister Abbey. Help may be at hand in the form of a handsome young traveller – but it's help at a price.

The Governess at St Agatha's by Yolanda Celbridge
March 1995   Price: £4.99   ISBN: 0 352 32986 6
A welcome return for Miss Constance de Comynge, former Cornish governess. Now she's headmistress of St Agatha's, a young ladies' academy where discipline is foremost on the syllabus. Competition is tough for places in the 'Swish Club', a select group whose beautiful members revel in punishing each other – and prominent members of the local gentry.

Western Star by Roxanne Carr
February 1995   Price: £4.99   ISBN: 0 352 32969 6
There's nothing for a spunky young woman in mid-19th-century Missouri, so Maribel Harker joins the wagon train to the bounteous West. Concerned, her father asks his trusted friend Dan Cutter to keep an eye on her. But with Maribel's looks and sexual appetite, no one could remain trusted for long.

A Private Collection by Sarah Fisher
February 1995   Price: £4.99   ISBN: 0 352 32970 X
Alicia Moffatt has an unusual boast: she is the owner of the most spectacular collection of erotica in the Western world. She engages a young writer to catalogue the works, but Franscesca soon finds out courtesy of Ms Moffatt's brawny chauffeur that games of depravity and voyeurism are not restricted to the books.

Unfinished Business by Sarah Hope-Walker
March 1995   Price: £4.99   ISBN: 0 352 32983 1
Joanne's job as financial analyst for a leading London bank requires a lot of responsibility and control. Her true, submissive self has little opportunity to blossom until the suave, gifted and dominant Nikolai walks into her life. But her happiness is soon threatened by the return of an equally masterful old flame.

Nicole's Revenge by Lisette Allen
March 1995   Price: £4.99   ISBN: 0 352 32984 X
It's taken Nicole Chabrier four years' hard work at the Paris Opera to make something of herself. But when France erupts into revolution, she has to rely on a dashing stranger to save her from an angry mob. She is only too happy to use her considerable charms to repay the favour and to help Jacques gain revenge on those who wronged him.

Nexus

NEXUS BACKLIST

Where a month is marked on the right, this book will not be published until that month in 1994. All books are priced £4.99 unless another price is given.

CONTEMPORARY EROTICA

CONTOURS OF DARKNESS	Marco Vassi		
THE DEVIL'S ADVOCATE	Anonymous		
THE DOMINO TATTOO	Cyrian Amberlake	£4.50	
THE DOMINO ENIGMA	Cyrian Amberlake		
THE DOMINO QUEEN	Cyrian Amberlake		
ELAINE	Stephen Ferris		
EMMA'S SECRET WORLD	Hilary James		
EMMA ENSLAVED	Hilary James		
FALLEN ANGELS	Kendal Grahame		
THE FANTASIES OF JOSEPHINE SCOTT	Josephine Scott		
THE GENTLE DEGENERATES	Marco Vassi		
HEART OF DESIRE	Maria del Rey		
HELEN – A MODERN ODALISQUE	Larry Stern		
HIS MISTRESS'S VOICE	G. C. Scott		Nov
THE HOUSE OF MALDONA	Yolanda Celbridge		Dec
THE INSTITUTE	Maria del Rey		
SISTERHOOD OF THE INSTITUTE	Maria del Rey		Sep
JENNIFER'S INSTRUCTION	Cyrian Amberlake		
MELINDA AND THE MASTER	Susanna Hughes		
MELINDA AND ESMERALDA	Susanna Hughes		
MELINDA AND THE COUNTESS	Susanna Hughes		Dec
MIND BLOWER	Marco Vassi		

MS DEEDES AT HOME	Carole Andrews	£4.50	
MS DEEDES ON PARADISE ISLAND	Carole Andrews		
THE NEW STORY OF O	Anonymous		
OBSESSION	Maria del Rey		
ONE WEEK IN THE PRIVATE HOUSE	Esme Ombreux		
THE PALACE OF FANTASIES	Delver Maddingley		
THE PALACE OF HONEYMOONS	Delver Maddingley		
THE PALACE OF EROS	Delver Maddingley		
PARADISE BAY	Maria del Rey		
THE PASSIVE VOICE	G. C. Scott		
THE SALINE SOLUTION	Marco Vassi		
STEPHANIE	Susanna Hughes		
STEPHANIE'S CASTLE	Susanna Hughes		
STEPHANIE'S REVENGE	Susanna Hughes		
STEPHANIE'S DOMAIN	Susanna Hughes		
STEPHANIE'S TRIAL	Susanna Hughes		
STEPHANIE'S PLEASURE	Susanna Hughes		Sep
THE TEACHING OF FAITH	Elizabeth Bruce		
THE TRAINING GROUNDS	Sarah Veitch		

EROTIC SCIENCE FICTION

ADVENTURES IN THE PLEASUREZONE	Delaney Silver	
RETURN TO THE PLEASUREZONE	Delaney Silver	
FANTASYWORLD	Larry Stern	Oct
WANTON	Andrea Arven	

ANCIENT & FANTASY SETTINGS

CHAMPIONS OF LOVE	Anonymous		
CHAMPIONS OF PLEASURE	Anonymous		
CHAMPIONS OF DESIRE	Anonymous		
THE CLOAK OF APHRODITE	Kendal Grahame		Nov
SLAVE OF LIDIR	Aran Ashe	£4.50	
DUNGEONS OF LIDIR	Aran Ashe		
THE FOREST OF BONDAGE	Aran Ashe	£4.50	
PLEASURE ISLAND	Aran Ashe		
WITCH QUEEN OF VIXANIA	Morgana Baron		

EDWARDIAN, VICTORIAN & OLDER EROTICA

ANNIE	Evelyn Culber	
ANNIE AND THE SOCIETY	Evelyn Culber	Oct
BEATRICE	Anonymous	
CHOOSING LOVERS FOR JUSTINE	Aran Ashe	
GARDENS OF DESIRE	Roger Rougiere	
THE LASCIVIOUS MONK	Anonymous	
LURE OF THE MANOR	Barbra Baron	
MAN WITH A MAID 1	Anonymous	
MAN WITH A MAID 2	Anonymous	
MAN WITH A MAID 3	Anonymous	
MEMOIRS OF A CORNISH GOVERNESS	Yolanda Celbridge	
TIME OF HER LIFE	Josephine Scott	
VIOLETTE	Anonymous	

THE JAZZ AGE

BLUE ANGEL DAYS	Margarete von Falkensee
BLUE ANGEL NIGHTS	Margarete von Falkensee
BLUE ANGEL SECRETS	Margarete von Falkensee
CONFESSIONS OF AN ENGLISH MAID	Anonymous
PLAISIR D'AMOUR	Anne-Marie Villefranche
FOLIES D'AMOUR	Anne-Marie Villefranche
JOIE D'AMOUR	Anne-Marie Villefranche
MYSTERE D'AMOUR	Anne-Marie Villefranche
SECRETS D'AMOUR	Anne-Marie Villefranche
SOUVENIR D'AMOUR	Anne-Marie Villefranche
WAR IN HIGH HEELS	Piers Falconer

SAMPLERS & COLLECTIONS

EROTICON 1	ed. J-P Spencer	
EROTICON 2	ed. J-P Spencer	
EROTICON 3	ed. J-P Spencer	
EROTICON 4	ed. J-P Spencer	
NEW EROTICA 1	ed. Esme Ombreux	
NEW EROTICA 2	ed. Esme Ombreux	
THE FIESTA LETTERS	ed. Chris Lloyd	£4.50

NON-FICTION

FEMALE SEXUAL AWARENESS	B & E McCarthy	£5.99
HOW TO DRIVE YOUR MAN WILD IN BED	Graham Masterton	
HOW TO DRIVE YOUR WOMAN WILD IN BED	Graham Masterton	
LETTERS TO LINZI	Linzi Drew	
LINZI DREW'S PLEASURE GUIDE	Linzi Drew	

Please send me the books I have ticked above.

Name ....

Address ....

....

....

.... Post code ....

Send to: Cash Sales, Nexus Books, 332 Ladbroke Grove, London W10 5AH.

Please enclose a cheque or postal order, made payable to **Nexus Books**, to the value of the books you have ordered plus postage and packing costs as follows:

UK and BFPO – £1.00 for the first book, 50p for each subsequent book.

Overseas (including Republic of Ireland) – £2.00 for the first book, £1.00 for the second book, and 50p for each subsequent book.

If you would prefer to pay by VISA or ACCESS/MASTERCARD, please write your card number and expiry date here:

....

Please allow up to 28 days for delivery.

Signature ....